DEW ON THE GRASS

Eiluned Lewis

Introduction by Dr Katie Gramich

ERRATUM

The name Llewellyn-Bowen on page 8 should read: Llewellyn Davies.

HONNO CLASSICS

Published by Honno
'Ailsa Craig', Heol y Cawl, Dinas Powys
South Glamorgan, Wales, CF6 4AH

Dew On The Grass was first published in 1934.
A second edition was published in 1984 by Boydell and Brewer Ltd.

The right of Eiluned Lewis to be identified a the author
of this work has been asserted in accordance with the
Copyright, Designs and Patents Act 1988

Published with the financial support of the Welsh Books Council

A catalogue record for this book
is available from The British Library.

ISBN 1 870206 800

Cover Image: Veer
Cover Design: Nicola Schumacher
Photographs by kind permission of Katrina Burnett,
from the estate of Eiluned Lewis

Printed in Wales by Gomer

CONTENTS

ERRATUM

The name Llewellyn-Bowen on
page 8 should read: Llewellyn
Davies.

INTRODUCTION

Eiluned Lewis (1900-1979)

Eiluned Lewis was born and brought up in the countryside near Newtown, Montgomeryshire on the cusp of the nineteenth and twentieth centuries. The Lewis family lived in the aptly-named 'Glan Hafren,' near the banks of 'the young Severn' as it is described in *Dew on the Grass*, her auto-biographical first novel. Eiluned was one of four children, with two sisters and a brother, exactly like Lucy, the protagonist of *Dew on the Grass*. Their parents were wealthy owners of land and a sheepskin tannery in the area, which was Hugh Lewis, their father's native place, though their mother, Eveline Lewis (neé Griffiths), came originally from Pembrokeshire and was a fluent Welsh-speaker. Eveline had been a county school headmistress before her marriage; the distant but adoring sketch of the mother rendered in *Dew on the Grass* suggests a highly cultured and charming woman. Both Eiluned's father and her brother, Peter, were strongly committed country sportsmen. Unusually for a woman even of her upper middle-class background, Eiluned gained an education at Westfield College at the University of London and thereafter worked as a personal assistant to newspaper director, Henry Cadbury, of the *Daily News* and later as a drama critic for the *Sunday Times*. In later life she wrote extensively for *Country Life* magazine.

She published three novels in all: *Dew on the Grass* (1934), *The Captain's Wife* (1943) and *The Leaves of the Tree* (1953). She was also a poet, publishing two volumes of verse, namely *December Apples* (1935) and *Morning Songs* (1944), as well as interpolating poems in her prose works. Her essays and rural sketches written for *Country Life* were collected in the volumes *In Country Places* (1951) and *Honey Pots and Brandy Bottles* (1954). Following her marriage to Graeme

Hendrey in 1937, she ceased to work as a Fleet Street journalist and returned both actually and in spirit to the rural world that she loved. Much of her later life was spent in Surrey, which forms the setting for her third novel, but both her first novels are set in Wales and it is clear that, despite living for many years in England, she continued in a sense to define herself as a Welsh writer, formed by her Montgomeryshire upbringing and her Pembrokeshire antecedents.

That 'Glan Hafren' in the early decades of the twentieth century was a cultured and cosmopolitan household is suggested by the fact that J. M. Barrie was a regular visitor, with his adoptive sons, the Llewellyn-Bowen boys, who participated in the home-devised amateur dramatics vividly evoked in *Dew on the Grass*. Later in life, Eiluned herself formed friendships with the Anglo-Welsh novelists Hilda Vaughan and her husband Charles Morgan. Eiluned edited a selection of Morgan's letters in 1967, with a memoir of her own which is also a tribute, possibly returning the favour Morgan had done her when he wrote a prefatory letter in praise of *Dew on the Grass*. Morgan was a highly regarded novelist in his day and his preface perhaps contributed something to the success enjoyed by Eiluned's first novel when it appeared in 1934. Indeed, for a first novel, the work was phenomenally successful, attracting positive reviews from literary critics, going rapidly through a number of editions, being translated into several other languages, and winning the Gold Medal of the Book Guild for the best novel of the year. When one thinks nowadays of a Welsh bestseller of the 1930s, it is inevitable that Richard Llewellyn's *How Green Was My Valley* comes to mind. However, *Dew on the Grass* predates Llewellyn's novel by five years and it is not inconceivable that Eiluned Lewis's runaway success with a novel of Welsh life may have encouraged Llewellyn to try his hand at a similar feat. In any case, the immediate appeal which ensured that Eiluned Lewis's first novel enjoyed such acclaim in its time is still tangible today from the very first, evocative and enticing pages of the book.

Literary contexts

Welsh fiction of the 1930s tends to be associated with male authors writing the industrial experience of the South Wales Valleys. There is a wealth of notable fiction from Wales in this period which, despite individual authors' stylistic and ideological differences, can be seen as representations of similar working-class, Welsh life. Examples of what we might call this school of writing are: Lewis Jones's recently republished novels, *Cwmardy* (1937) and *We Live* (1939), the autobiographical writings of the collier Bert Coombes, including *These Poor Hands* (1939), Gwyn Thomas's early Rhondda fiction, such as *Sorrow for thy Sons* (written 1937; published 1986), Rhys Davies's Welsh comedies of manners, with their dark undertones of sexual transgression, such as *Jubilee Blues* (1938), Gwyn Jones's realistic account of the Depression in *Times Like These* (1936), Jack Jones's many semi-autobiographical fictions including *Rhondda Roundabout* (1934) and, of course, Richard Llewellyn's aforementioned bestseller, *How Green Was My Valley* (1939). The single female author of the period who is occasionally discussed alongside the chroniclers of the industrial experience is the Welsh-language writer, Kate Roberts, whose novel *Traed mewn Cyffion* (1936; translated as *Feet in Chains,* 1977) is set in the slate-quarrying community of North-West Wales between 1880 and the middle of the First World War. Roberts's moving text actually sits rather uneasily alongside the novels of her male contemporaries, not only by virtue of its different language and setting but also in its distinct representations of gender, domesticity, culture and politics. One noteworthy difference between Kate Roberts's work and that of her South Welsh peers is that the setting of her novel is actually a rural, small-farming environment, despite the area's economic dependence on the slate-quarrying industry. Small-scale farming is a necessary supplement to the quarryman's wages in every family. The children in the novel – and there is significant focus on the child's experience – spend much of their time out of doors, on the mountainsides. Children are important in Kate Roberts's fictional world in a way which distinguishes it fundamentally from the primary focus on the adult working man's perspective in many of her male contemporaries' writing. Nevertheless, the perspective in Kate Roberts's novel is predominantly that of the mother of the family, Jane Gruffydd. Eiluned Lewis in her novel of the 1930s, *Dew on the Grass* (1934) shares with Kate Roberts a concern with gender, domesticity, Welsh culture and the rural environment, but she shifts the perspective squarely from the mother to the female child. Indeed, both mother and father are very much background figures in Lewis's fictional world, where the norm, the central consciousness is that of the child.

It would be inaccurate to suggest that child protagonists are absent from the works of male Welsh writers of the thirties, however. Rhys Davies memorably adopts the naïve perspective of a child in a number of his short stories, such as 'The Funeral' (1936) and the later story 'The Fashion Plate' (1949). This strategy is used by Davies to reveal the cruelty of the adult world, creating poignancy in the fact that the sensitive child will soon have to survive in that unforgiving place. Dylan Thomas's use of child narrators and protagonists is also marked but very different. In stories such as 'A Visit to Grandpa's'(1938) and Extraordinary Little Cough'(1939), as well as better-known texts such as 'The Peaches' (1938) and the later 'A Child's Christmas in Wales'(1945), Thomas re-enters a child's imaginative realm with all its terrors and enthusiasms. There is, however, a definite nostalgia in Thomas's evocation of childhood which does not always escape sentimentality. Eiluned Lewis's tour-de-force of recreating a child's world-view in *Dew on the Grass* is tonally similar to Dylan Thomas, though her work in this mode pre-dates his by several years. As in Thomas, there is in Eiluned Lewis's child-world a sense of nostalgia, an acute sense of the extremes of passion and emotion experienced by the child, a sense of questioning and frequent bewilderment at the inexplicable rituals of adulthood, as well as a lively sense of humour and incongruity. Like Thomas's, Lewis's child-world is not pure idyll but a place of imagination and delight hedged around with menace, punishment and disappointment. Also like Thomas, Lewis occasionally hovers on the edge of sentimentality but her astute sense of structure allows her to introduce a laconic contrast just when the child narrative threatens to become twee.

Beyond the context of Welsh writing, Lewis's child-centred narrative inevitably brings to mind the short stories of Katherine Mansfield. There are strong similarities between Lewis's representation of children and that of Mansfield, including a feeling of longing and a vivid evocation of fear and death in the child's otherwise innocent world. Lewis's Lucy is reminiscent of Mansfield's Kezia in 'Prelude' (1917) and 'At the Bay'(1921) and the description of the bucolic summers of childhood in both writers' works points to the common autobiographical impulse underpinning them.

Nor is Mansfield's Modernism irrelevant to a consideration of Lewis's style. Writing only a decade or so after authors such as Mansfield and Woolf experimented with stream-of-consciousness narrative, Lewis tempers her detailed realism with a strong internal monologue on the part of eight-year-old Lucy and frequently blurs the boundaries between the 'real' external world and the more extravagant world of Lucy's imagination. This willingness to experiment with narrative results in a fluid and compelling prose which avoids the tedium of indefatigable documentary realism and the self-indulgent excesses of exuberant symbolism.

But if certain aspects of Lewis's style show the influence of Modernist experimentation, the dominant tone is undoubtedly Romantic. Irene Walters has pointed out in her research on Lewis that the Gwyn children of Pengarth seem to echo the Romantic grouping of the Brontës of Haworth: three sisters and a brother in a remote rural landscape, who spend their time inventing and inhabiting imaginary worlds. Walters also notes that, like the Brontës' Gondal and Angria, Lucy's imaginary world is also reigned over by powerful queens (alter egos of the children themselves).

Clearly, it is no accident either that the main protagonist of *Dew on the Grass* is named 'Lucy'. The Romantic attachment to the natural world evinced in the novel is reminiscent of the work of Wordsworth, also known for his championing of the child and for his poignant series of 'Lucy poems'. Wordsworth's Lucy is already dead and evoked nostalgically and longingly in verse of beautiful simplicity. In a sense, one might argue that Eiluned Lewis's Lucy, too, is now dead: she is the child self of years ago, living in a turn-of-the-century Welsh rural world which by 1934 already seemed like another country. Yet Lucy Gwyn lives on with extraordinary vividness in the author's memory and imagination, just as Wordsworth's Lucy lives in his poems, evoking 'joy! That in our embers/Is something that doth live,/That nature yet remembers/What was so fugitive!' ('Ode: Intimations of Immortality,' 1807) Eiluned Lewis's novel may be seen as an embodiment of Wordsworth epigraph to the 'Immortality Ode': 'The Child is father of the Man;/And I could wish my days to be/Bound each to each in natural piety,' except that Lewis changes the gender of the Child: her 'Lucy' is mother of the Woman and Author.

Gender and Authorship

Despite the efforts of Louisa the nursemaid to domesticate Lucy, she is very reluctant to take on a conventionally obedient, feminine role. The episodic structure of the novel reveals Lucy again and again transgressing the rules governing 'proper' behaviour for a girl and subsequently receiving punishment for her transgression at Louisa's hands. It is Lucy's elder sister, Delia, who takes on the role of the properly domesticated little girl; when, at the end of the novel, Delia is sent away to boarding school, Lucy comes to the awful realization that she herself, now, must step into Delia's shoes: 'with Delia's going something far more serious had happened, for now she must put away her "other" life.'(p. 220) Lucy's "other" life is her life as an Author, creator and manipulator of a rich fictional world. Her siblings also participate in this world: Maurice, Lucy's brother, likes playing with dolls but knows that as a boy he is not allowed to *except* in their imaginary world. Lucy realizes that the 'make-believe world' affords them a freedom from the limiting gender constraints of the real world: 'when Maurice … said "Pretend I'm not a boy!" he was immediately free to play at tea-parties to his heart's content.' (p. 201) Similarly, when Lucy is left to her own devices, she takes on the role of 'Hawk-eye' from her favourite book, *The Last of the Mohicans* and her stereotypically masculine task is 'rescuing the ladies Cora and Alice from the Huron tribe.' (p. 104) However, by the end of the novel she and her playmate David begin to show awareness of gender difference: on their last day together before he, too, is sent away to school, while he fashions a boat out of plasticine, she makes a teapot. Lewis's approach to gender is implicitly critical but also, finally, resigned to the inevitable. As Wordsworth puts it:

'Full soon thy soul shall have her earthly freight,
And custom lie upon thee with a weight,
Heavy as frost, and deep almost as life!'
(Immortality Ode)

Class

One of the most striking ways in which Eiluned Lewis's novel differs from those of many of her Welsh contemporaries is in its focus on upper middle-class life, rather than the working-class focus of the majority of her peers.   Even some of Eiluned's female contemporaries from not dissimilar class backgrounds, such as Hilda Vaughan and Margiad Evans, frequently focus on working-class rural life, such as in Evans's *Country Dance* (1932) or Vaughan's *A Thing of Nought* (1934). Their precursor, Allen Raine, though like Hilda Vaughan the daughter of a country solicitor, also focused her attention primarily on working-class characters in rural Cardiganshire. It was almost as if these middle-class Welsh writers hesitated to turn the spotlight on their own class and its mores. In Eiluned Lewis's novel, however, Lucy's family, the Gwyns, are Anglo-Welsh landed gentry, as was Lewis's own family; the Gwyns' estate appears to be extensive, including a number of farms and cottages with dependent tenants and Pengarth, the 'home-farm' is run by a large complement of servants. Lucy and her three siblings have a formidable nursemaid called Louisa, and there is in addition Bessie and Jane the housemaids, Dick the stable-boy, Davey John the farm labourer, Sarah the parlour-maid, Mrs Banister the cook, Twm the gamekeeper, and Beedles the coachman.

The family has a close and friendly relationship with the servants but there is a definite sense of social hierarchy, reflected for instance in the fact that Denis the hay-cutter refers to the children deferentially as '*Miss* Daylia and *Miss* Lucy' (p. 45). Lucy is largely unaware of class distinctions, however, living as she does in perpetual fear of retribution by her stern Welsh nurse, Louisa. There are indications that poverty and want exist in this society but, interestingly, these occur towards the end of the novel, reflecting Lucy's growing awareness of the adult world around her. In Chapter sixteen, for example, the Gwyns visit Martha Hamer and her seven children in their tiny cottage 'which smelt hot and damp, like the ironing room at Pengarth.' (p. 190)

Lucy has a number of encounters with figures who lie on the margins of the class system and, interestingly, she identifies with them and seems to be acknowledged by them as a kindred spirit. She meets the gipsy, Ned Lovell, who teaches her how to fish and for whose 'heady companionship' she is willing to suffer 'retribution – Louisa and dry bread for supper.'(p. 54) Later, she meets Billy Bennett the poacher, who carries a ferret in a bag and is allegedly looking for 'oonts' (moles); he kindly gives her the mushrooms he has picked to replace the blackberries she has managed to spill while falling into a bog. These poacher characters actually disrupt the system on which the Gwyn estate is built but Lucy is fascinated by these outsiders and their life of freedom. There is certainly no critique of the class system in the novel but, through Lucy's consciousness, there is a sense that some of its rigid demarcations of 'good' (Louisa) and 'bad' (Billy Bennett) are at least questionable.

Most poignant of all in terms of Lucy's encounters with outsiders in the novel is concerned, is her meeting with the unnamed tramp in Chapter eighteen. She and the rector's son, David, are playing in the cemetery, where there is a newly-opened grave and they are interrupted by the arrival of a strange man. Echoes of the opening chapter of Dickens's *Great Expectations* are inevitably created as the man asks for food and boots but the menace created by Magwitch never materialises here and the man is seen, through Lucy's eyes, as a pitiful and poignant figure. It is a tangible eruption of history into the timeless world of Pengarth, for the tramp is a refugee from the industrial unrest and poverty of the South Wales Valleys. As he himself says, bridling at the rude label of 'tramp' that David assigns him: '"Oh, it's tramps, is it?...What right 'ave you got to call me names, I'd like ter know, if an honest man can't get work? Why don't you blame the rotten country? 'Aven't I walked all the way from Cardiff? And the bloody Unions taking it out of a chap till you might as well be dead, I tell you, dead and rotted and shovelled away in there." He nodded at the grave.' (p. 209) In a rather inadequate gesture of sympathy, Lucy gives the man a slice of bread and treacle and he goes on his way. Yet the encounter remains in Lucy's mind as a disquieting omen that she will soon be entering that adult world of injustice and pain.

Religion

If one of the enduring and distinctive features of Welsh women's writing until very recent years has been its concern with religion and religious experience, Eiluned Lewis emphatically reveals her Welsh credentials in this novel. Its title is an echo of a verse from the Old Testament and the text is littered with Biblical allusions and quotations. The verse from Proverbs which gives the novel its title is, in the King James version: 'The king's wrath is as the roaring of a lion; but his favour is as dew upon the grass.'(*Proverbs* Chapter 19, verse 12) This evocative verse conjures up the extremes of the child's world: Lucy and her siblings live in a Welsh rural environment which seems blessed with the favour of the Creator whose generosity and beneficence is rendered in the image of dew upon the grass. But the other – unquoted – element of the verse suggests the ever-lurking danger of incurring the wrath of the Old Testament God who is as dangerous and destructive as the marauding wild beast. It is between these extremes of beatitude and terror that the child's life is lived.

Lucy and her siblings, despite their youth, are connoisseurs of sermons, showing a decided preference for the 'hwyl' of the chapel minister's Welsh over the dull dutifulness of the Anglican vicar's English, although they can scarcely understand the language of the former. Lucy herself 'was always expecting God to call her, as He had called the Infant Samuel.' (p. 26) Her early ambition is to be a hymn-writer, surely a very Welsh choice of vocation for a little girl. She is entranced by Biblical language, which echoes through her active imagination, though she often has at best a hazy idea of the meaning of the words themselves. Thus, the phrase 'carnally minded' appeals to her ear, though ironically she has as yet no conception of what the phrase denotes. Lucy is drawn to theological speculation; her favourite pastime is to lie in a hammock and think about death and religion.

In fact death is a constant preoccupation: many of the stories she invents about imaginary characters, such as the 'Innocent Child'(p. 37), the 'Toothless Hag' and the 'Armenians' (p. 38) involve torture and horrid death. It is almost as if, when she becomes an Author, she emulates the Old Testament Creator and wreaks her wrath upon her creations. [Interestingly, however, there is a vague hint of historical consciousness in Lucy's choice of the 'Armenians' as heroes of her stories since, although the setting of the novel pre-dates the genocide suffered by the Armenians during World War I, at the turn of the century they were already a small *Christian* people, persecuted both by the Russians and by the ruling Ottomans.]

The children attend church regularly, occasionally the Welsh chapel, and also study the Bible at home. They mimic the ecclesiastical rituals in their home-devised funeral services for dead animals. This, too, leads to theological debate about whether animals possess souls. When Lucy visits a farm on her father's estate, she notices a sampler on the kitchen wall, which reads 'Martha Jane Gethin. Fear the Lord. 1874.' (p. 142) along with a print of Daniel in the Lion's den. This juxtaposition again brings to mind the verse from *Proverbs* which gives the novel its title: Lucy's world is ruled by a Creator who must be feared yet who is also capable of great tenderness.

Wales and Welsh identity

It is clear from the loving opening description of the site of Pengarth, on the Welsh side of 'the young Severn' that Lewis's characters usually define themselves as Welsh and significantly different from their English neighbours. The mother of the family is a Welsh-speaking Pembrokeshire woman, as is the grandmother, who visits and teaches the children verses in Welsh. Moreover, aunt Shân lives in a west Wales seaside resort recognizable as Aberdovey, where the children are immersed in a more intensively Welsh-speaking environment for part of the summer. Characters and places are marked by their distinctively Welsh names, even if sometimes rendered in an Anglicised form, such as 'Twm the Weeg' (=[G]wig, meaning wood). Nevertheless, the Gwyns are typical Anglo-Welsh gentry of the period (c. 1908) in that they ensure that their children receive a thoroughly English education. Before they are packed off to boarding school in England, the children are subjected to the ministrations of Miss Crabtree, who 'came on a bicycle three mornings a week to teach arithmetic, grammar and the Kings of England.'(p. 45). Yet Louisa, the Gwyns' nursemaid, is clearly a Welsh-speaker and a devout chapel-goer. The text is sprinkled with approximations of her Welsh exclamations, such as 'caudle' (=cawdel, meaning 'mess' and 'nem-o-dear' (presumably a corruption of 'yn enw Duw', in the name of God). Other servants and tenants are also Welsh-speakers, such as Davey John, the farm worker, who calls the children 'bach' and is fond of the exclamation 'Jowks' (a version of the Welsh swear word 'diawl', meaning 'the devil'). But this is the time of the heyday of the British Empire, as evidenced in Delia's pencil-box, which bears 'a picture of Lord Kitchener on the lid,' (p. 46) and they all intone 'a prayer for the King.' (p. 61). The children's father recites Gray's 'Elegy' to them, while aunt Shân's house in Aberdovey contains just four books: 'two bound volumes of the *Ladies' Magazine*;

Dickens's *Christmas Carol*; *Tristan and Iseult* in green suède, and *Scenes from Clerical Life*.' (p. 78) This is indistinguishable from a bourgeois English household of the period and yet the girls are bewitched by the fact that in Shân's house 'after you had gone to bed you could hear the swish and slap of waves, and the noise of people walking to and fro and talking in Welsh,' (p. 69) The children have a copy of *Little Arthur's England* in the nursery and a painting of 'An English Farm Yard' hanging in their bedroom in Shân's house (p. 84). And yet Lucy, when she holds forth to Davey John about the probability that ' Henry VII …came through this field on his way to the Battle of Bosworth', urges 'wouldn't you like to have been there, marching into England with a Welsh army?' (p. 109) Lucy's political allegiances, such as they are, are clear. Similarly, in Chapter 11, when the traditional Welsh harpist, John Roberts, comes to play on their lawn, Lucy responds intensely to this 'different music: it came from everywhere, and yet from nowhere…and at the same time it came from inside Lucy's own head, so that she knew that this was the music for which she had always been waiting.' (p. 121) The music the harpist plays is Welsh folk music, such as 'Hob-y-deri-dando', 'Bugeilio'r Gwenith Gwyn' and 'David of the White Rock.' (p. 122)

The Gwyns' Wales is defined by its rurality and by its relatively static social hierarchy. South Wales is, for the Gwyn children at least, an alien place. Lucy is startled by the tramp from Cardiff because he speaks differently and displays an anger at injustice which is new to her. When the family travels to aunt Shân's house in West Wales, they hear the porters in the railway station shout "Change here for South Wales!" and Lucy reflects wonderingly that 'there actually is a train waiting to go to South Wales – that unknown country – and people strolling unconcernedly to catch it.' (p. 67)

Dew on the Grass, then, presents an ostensibly contradictory representation of Welsh identity. While the Welsh language and aspects of Welsh culture such as music, poetry, and religion, are certainly presented in a positive way, these markers of Welshness are incorporated within a dominant social identity defined by Britishness and class allegiance. There are moreover indications that the new sense of working-class identity which was historically crystallising in the South Wales Valleys at the time is viewed as something threatening and alien. Lucy is acutely aware that the tramp's accent sounds 'quite different from the voices of the people who lived in Pengarth.' (p. 209) This 'difference' has underlying political implications which as it were force themselves into a text which is trying to avoid them; while the Welsh servants and tenants of Pengarth are apparently content with their station, the tramp's voice is the rumbling murmur of social change which will soon threaten and destroy the stable world of Pengarth forever and will, at the same time, lead to a new, and politicised, form of Welsh identity.

Katie Gramich, *July 2006*

BIBLIOGRAPHY

Cavaliero, Glen, Introduction to *Dew on the Grass* by Eiluned Lewis (Woodbridge: Boydell and Brewer, 1984)

Lewis, Eiluned, *The Captain's Wife* (London: Macmillan, 1943)

Lewis, Eiluned, *The Leaves of the Tree* (London: Peter Davies, 1953)

Lewis, Eiluned, ed., *Selected Letters of Charles Morgan* (London: Macmillan, 1967)

Lewis, Eiluned, A Companionable Talent: Stories, Essays and Recollections, ed., Glen Cavaliero (Goudhurst, Finchcocks Press, 1996)

Walters, Irene, *Facing Annihilation: Genre, Gender and Social Issues in the Works of Eiluned Lewis*, (unpublished MA thesis, Trinity College, Carmarthen, 1998)

We who were born
In country places,
Far from cities
And shifting faces,
We have a birthright
No man can sell,
And a secret joy
No man can tell.

For we are kindred
To lordly things:
The wild duck's flight
And the white owl's wings,
To pike and salmon,
To bull and horse,
The curlew's cry
And the smell of gorse.

Pride of trees,
Swiftness of streams,
Magic of frost
Have shaped our dreams.
No baser vision
Their spirit fills
Who walk by right
On the naked hills.

Chapter One

Pengarth

A stranger, crossing the valley from north to south, searching for ford or footbridge over the young Severn, would come suddenly upon Pengarth and might wonder—if his sense of direction were confused—to which point of the compass the river was flowing. For it so winds and wanders, looping the fields and threading the tangled trees with S-shaped curves, that it seems in two minds whether to make its way into England or return to the hills. Embracing the last inch of orchard and hayfield, it turns at length reluctantly towards the east, the widening valley and the fat water-meadows.

Having settled this matter of geography, the stranger, still resting on a foothill above Pengarth, might ask himself if the scatter of roofs, chimneys and weathervanes behind the house were not a small hamlet; and decide that, if they were no more than outbuildings, the house to which they belonged, almost hidden by trees, must be a place of some importance.

Here again he would need to correct his first impression, for there was a sense of space, order and dignity about the Pengarth outbuildings which was lacking in the house. Perhaps the old place had seen too many changes to feel that dignity mattered greatly. Six hundred years had passed since it was built as a farm-house. Under the oak beams of the original kitchen, salmon, fresh-caught from the river, had been smoked, to be carried for sale on horseback into England. Succeeding generations of farmers and small gentry had added to the house, here a storey and there a room, heedless of symmetry or foundations, so that on stormy nights, when the wind rushed through the keyhole of the hills, walls rocked, joists groaned and cracks widened ominously in

the plaster. There were rooms into which you stepped
suddenly up or down, floors that sloped like a hillside,
ceilings elaborately ornamented with plaster scrolls and
flowers, and others so low that no one above the age of ten
could stand upright in them. Between the walls were spaces,
large enough to hide a dozen men, where birds entered and
flapped dismally in the dark. No one could tell how they came
in, and they themselves had lost the way out.

But the man who built the outhouses planned them all in a
piece and with an eye to what was required of a gentleman.
The grey stone saddle-room, with its leaded windows, was
lofty and raftered like a church. Above the long line of
coachhouses, loose-box, washhouse, bottle-room and granary
stood a gilded weathervane on a bell-tower; the apple-loft,
with its stone steps and pointed roof, wore a faintly
ecclesiastical air, and the spreading barns, cow-houses, wood-
shed, pigstyes and dog-kennels, the walled kitchen garden
with its stone sundial, its ample potting-shed and greenhouse
suggested complacent dignity and infinite leisure.

Round the house grew a tangle of trees and shrubs.
Beeches, sycamores and oaks stood sentinel outside the
windows; rhododendrons, laurustinus and variegated hollies
crept round the walls and ran riot on the lawns and river bank.
When John Gwyn came to Pengarth, as a young bachelor, he
ordered the shrubs to be trimmed and left everything else as
he found it; but a few years later, when he brought his bride to
the house and the stable bell was rung in her honour, the lady
wept to see so many bushes. She had come from a treeless
county of wide horizons and never grew quite used to the
restricted outlook, even when her husband pulled up half the
shrubbery and obligingly lopped the lower branches of the
trees. Yet they loved each other so much that no amount of
vegetation could smother their happiness.

The names of their four children, who grew up at Pengarth,
were recorded by a pencilled legend on the stable door of

stout oak. It ran "Delia, Lucy, Maurice (in boots), Miriam (barefoot)"—being a memorial of the height of the young Gwyns at the time of this story.

Delia, aged eleven, topped the list, with Lucy two years younger. Maurice, aged six, who had stoutly refused to remove his boots, came some way below, and Miriam—who ran to width rather than height—barely managed to reach the key-hole at three and a half years.

Beetles, the coachman, measured them all. It was he who noticed that Lucy's curls, which grew upright, were adding an inch to her stature and flattened them out with the stable brush.

Chapter Two

Hide and Seek

The Rectory children had come to tea and now all of them had run out into the garden and were deciding what game they should play next. Released at length from the spell of Louisa's eye and the cool, leafshaded nursery, they danced out on the lawn, shouting, hopping with excitement, ready for something adventurous, scarcely able to contain their glee.

"Rounders!" someone shouted. But were there enough of them for rounders? Yes, if they got Dick the stableboy to join in; then Delia remembered that Dick was cleaning out the hen-house under Jarman's eye, so it was no use counting on him.

"Hide and seek!" called out David. "I vote for hide and seek."

"No, no, not hide and seek," Lucy thought to herself. "Oh, God," she prayed rapidly—half shutting her eyes because you should always pray with your eyes closed, but only half because the others might notice and laugh at her—"let it not be hide and seek. Please, dear God, let it not be hide and seek."

But it was. Perhaps God didn't mind what game they played, although it mattered so much to Lucy; or perhaps He was punishing her for being rude to Louisa that morning.

Now they were picking up sides—David and Delia calling out names. If David did not choose her, Delia of course would not do so until the end when there was no one else left, because you did not choose your own sister when there were guests present, and to be left till the end was a kind of disgrace. But David did choose her. "I'll have Lucy," he said. Stepping calmly across to stand by his side, that was thrilling;

better than anything else in the world—like joining the Young Pretender; or the prophet in the Bible who called out, "Who is on the Lord's side?"

The sycamore tree was Home, and when they had tossed a threepenny-bit of David's which he took airily from his pocket, as though he were quite used to carrying money about with him, as well as marbles and putty and a two-bladed knife, it fell so that Delia's side should hide first. Perhaps God had been attending after all, for seeking was not nearly so bad as hiding.

David counted a hundred, in tens, rapidly to himself on his fingers, which was perhaps hardly fair, since it does not take so long as saying numbers like seventyfive out aloud. Then he yelled "Coming!" and paused only long enough to direct operations. Peggy and Lena were despatched to the stables and kitchengarden; Lucy was to search the nut bushes down the bank and along the hedge where the rabbits and guineapigs lay buried beneath green mounds. "And keep near Home," David shouted after her; "you're quick on your feet and that's where you'll be useful."

Lucy held her chin in the air; David had said she was "quick on her feet"; he had chosen her above his sisters for a responsible position.

Nobody in the nut bushes, nor behind the great holly tree at the wicket-gate. To go through it into the orchard would be disobeying David, so she climbed up the bank again and there was Delia's white frock fluttering on the edge of the tennis lawn. Lucy set off in pursuit and then she heard David's voice shouting: "Don't go after her. Keep back towards Home."

So she kept back and suddenly out of the rhododendron bushes burst Olwen, her black hair streaming in the wind. Lucy was so near to her now that she could hear her pant; out of the corner of her eye she saw that Delia was trying to dodge David on the tennis lawn, their fleetness well matched, but poor Olwen in her tight pink cotton dress and with her fat

legs in black woollen stockings could not hold out much
longer. Lucy touched her, screaming with excitement, just as
Delia jumped the tennis net and got home with David at her
heels, and Lena and Peggy came shouting to say that they had
cornered Maurice behind the cowhouse door. He trotted
behind them, a little disconsolate, but preoccupied as usual
with his own affairs.

Now it was their turn to hide: now Lucy must face it, this
thing that she dreaded so much. Her prayers had availed
nothing. The other side were under the sycamore tree, hiding
their eyes; David, Lena, Peggy and Lucy tiptoeing across the
lawn. The sun was still shining, just as it had been when
David had praised her running and she had been so happy; but
now she was wretched.

Lena and Peggy whispered together and disappeared into
the shrubbery; David nodded to Lucy and jumped the railings
into the paddock; she had half hoped that he would say she
might come with him, but now she must go on alone. Hiding
was bad enough, waiting behind a door, holding your breath,
fearing that a groping hand might suddenly touch you, a
triumphant voice shriek, "Here she is!" But how much worse
were the flight and pursuit: feet running behind, drawing
nearer every minute. Useless to say that this was only
Maurice or Delia after you, worse than useless, because at
bottom you knew that it was something really dreadful,
something infinitely disastrous that would catch you in the
end, however fast you ran.

It was the same when she and Maurice played trains
together with flags made from pieces of stuff nailed to pea-
sticks. The red flag meant "Stop!", and the green one "Go
on!", but there was also a yellow one made from a scrap of
yellow print left over from one of Delia's summer frocks.
With this they had invented for themselves the signal "Come
to me!", which gave a pleasant variety to the game until one

day Lucy, who was the guard, with Maurice as engine, lost the red flag. (They found it later in the asparagus bed.)

"Stop," she shouted, when Maurice came whistling and puffing up the garden path, digging his toes into the ground so that the pebbles were scattered in small showers. "Can't," he said laconically. "Not till you wave the red flag."

"But I can't find it," she cried, wildly waving the yellow one.

"Then I shall go on coming to you," and he went on doggedly, puffing and whistling and drawing nearer every minute, even when the guard took to her heels in panic. They ran round and round the walled kitchen garden; only when she was finally cornered in the potting-shed and had flung the yellow flag from her did the inexorable engine apply its brakes.

"What did you think would really happen to you," he asked, roused for once from his own imaginings by her white face and obvious distress. She could not explain; but nothing would ever induce her to play the game again.

Now she must find a place to hide in before Delia should have finished counting a hundred. Delia counted slowly and honourably, yet even now they might be upon her, with the cover of the shrubbery left behind. Rapidly she ran through the best places of concealment. There was the potato-house: few people would think of looking there; on the other hand, if they did (and Delia had a way of reading her thoughts) she would be caught like a mouse in a trap in that dark place, smelling of earth, with no more than a streak of yellow daylight showing through the crack in the door. Compared with the potato-house the tool-shed offered more possibilities, since you could escape to the rear through the door into the rick-yard. But this strategy had been used too often; Delia, who was a canny general, would be sure to think of it, sending Maurice or Olwen round to cut off retreat.

There was, she considered, the apple-room, a pleasant,

sweet-smelling place where the sun filtered through on to rows of green and rosy apples, reached by a flight of stone steps, slippery with moss. Chased up those steps once by David, Lucy had taken a flying leap from the top, jumping into a heap of dead leaves and broken wine-bottles beneath. She had been badly cut, and hide and seek was forbidden for a whole week afterwards. No, not the apple-room to-day, she decided.

By this time she had reached the stable-yard; in the distance behind her she heard Delia's shrill cry of "Coming!", and at that she slipped into the coachhouse and up the stairs into the loft.

Now the children's father had issued orders that no one was to climb those stairs because the roof above the coach-house was unsafe, so that a disobedient child might at any moment be precipitated with a cascade of outworn lath and plaster on to the brougham or dogcart below, or even on to grandmother's phaeton, shrouded in dust-sheets, its upturned shafts mutely imploring. Here then was a place which not even the wise Delia or crafty Olwen would think of searching. Holding her breath, Lucy stepped lightly across the forbidden territory, an overturned garden-seat and a disused pair of oars looming in the half-light, pushed open the door beyond and stepped into the granary: only when she had closed and bolted the heavy oak door behind her did she breathe freely.

The granary reminded her of church: there was the same raftered roof and a window cut into small, heavily-leaded panes, high up in the wall. By standing tiptoe on a corn-bin she could see through it, and there far below were the corner of the paddock and the place where the mown grass was tipped in a green pile, and the white door into the kitchen garden: yet seen from here all these things were bright, shining, unfamiliar, like the world when you stooped down and looked at it backwards between your legs; or like a day when Louisa was not in one of her scolding moods.

That day had begun badly, but as soon as the Rectory children came to tea everything was all right, and there was Louisa in her starchy, clean apron and cap, sitting behind the blue teapot and talking as though her mouth were suddenly full of plums. "Now, Master David, will you have some jam sandwich?" "Pass the bread and butter to Miss Olwen, Lucy." "Have you seen our new kittens, Miss Lena? They're such pretty little things."

How round and still the world seemed then! The blue rim on the nursery tea-service was a circle that enclosed it, and safe inside were the dim room shadowed with leaves, the white cloth, the sound of woodpigeons in the garden, the pattern in the branches of the trees which Lucy could see from her place at table, and Louisa and she on good terms with each other.

Louisa was really very kind at times, Lucy thought, settling herself comfortably on the corn-bin. For instance, she had not laughed at all when she discovered that Lucy was always expecting God to call her, as He had called the Infant Samuel. For a long time, after hearing that story, Lucy went about listening, and when, as sometimes happened, she fancied she heard a voice she would stand still and with closed eyes and clasped hands repeat the words: "Speak, Lord; for Thy servant heareth." Sometimes the voice turned out to be her mother calling to Beedles; on one occasion it was Louisa herself: "Didn't you hear me," she asked angrily when Lucy, realising that the call was not, after all, from Heaven, had come reluctantly in from the garden. "Why didn't you come at once?" Something prompted Lucy to tell. (Oh, how awful if David and Delia were to find out! How they would laugh at her!) Yet, because there had been so many disappointments, because she despaired of God's ever really wanting her, she had blurted out the truth to Louisa, and Louisa had suddenly enfolded her in her arms.

"Nem-o-dear! You do get some old-fashioned notions, to be sure!"

After that she had given up listening for God's voice, but now in the remote and silent granary, with the sound of voices calling in the distance, she fell to thinking of Him once more and decided that this would be a very good place in which to play at Church. Delia would be the congregation, a part she acted with great spirit, kneeling with fervently bent head or leaning forward from the waist, according to the character she represented. Maurice would be the organist, pulling out the stops of an invisible harmonium, and Lucy would preach the sermon and compose the hymns—both words and music. She began to invent one now, and was rather pleased with the result:

> "Think, think, think,,
> Of all the wrong you've done,
> Think, think, think,
> Of all the wrong you've done,
> Think, think, think . . ."

When she grew up, she decided, she would write hymns which people would print with her name at the end, and after it the date on which she was born, as they did in Louisa's chapel hymn-book. At first this would be followed with a dash and a blank, but after she was dead there would be the date on which she died, and when Louisa herself sang the hymns in her strong, trilling voice she would remember Lucy and perhaps the tears would come into her eyes at the thought of all the times she had scolded her. That, Lucy reflected, would be very satisfactory.

When she had considered this for some time, she stood up on the bin and looked out of the window once more. The paddock lay striped with long shadows and the rooks were cawing in the tree-tops; the voices that she had heard calling now called again; perhaps it really was God this time, but she did not feel sure, she felt even a little uncomfortable—it was very like Louisa's voice. Others joined in: there was no doubt now about its being Louisa, and Beedles as well. They were talking together, but Lucy could not hear what they said. Then she heard the bolt move in the coach-house door and Beedles's heavy footsteps coming upstairs.

They had found her after all; but why had Beedles, who was always too grumpy to play at anything, joined in the game? He was shouting now from the bottom of the stairs: "You up there, Miss Lucy?"

Should she jump into one of the bins? But there might be a rat inside. Or climb out of-the window? But it was too high to reach, and outside it were only the slippery slates and a sheer drop into the stableyard beneath. Beedles was crossing the loft now, stumbling over the oars, grumbling at his rheumatics. "Drat that child!" she heard him mutter, his hand fumbling at the door. Lucy thought of Catherine Douglas who thrust her arm into the door as a bolt, but then there was a king in hiding; and this wasn't the kind of door where you could thrust your arm in anywhere, and anyway it was too late.

"Well, I never did!" said Beedles. "You do beat all. Whatever are you a-doing of?" Then he turned and shouted down the stairs. "Here she be, Louisa, right enough."

"But why are you playing hide and seek, Beedles?" asked Lucy.

"That's what I'd like to know," he answered sourly "Come on down now, and mind where you're stepping."

"But where are David and all the others?"

"Gone home long ago, and I'd have gone too if Louisa hadn't been crazy looking for you."

"Is she very angry?" asked Lucy in a small voice.

"She's in a regular tantrum, I reckon. But don't you be a-feared. I'll talk her round."

Louisa was very cross—and with good reason. The Rectory children had all gone home long ago and Maurice and little Miriam were already in bed; even Delia was sitting in front of the nursery window having her long, shining hair brushed by Bessie the housemaid, while Louisa searched the garden and outhouses for Lucy. There was no jam or butter for her supper that evening.

Afterwards, when they were both in bed, Lucy confided to Delia the first verse of her new hymn:

"Think, think, think,
            Of all the wrong you've done . . .

But I can't find a good last line," she added.

"Like currants in a bun," said Delia practically. It did not seem quite right. Lucy was aware of a drop in the poetic temperature, but, as usual, Delia had settled the matter. After all, sins werc rather like currants, since they were many and black, and of a pleasant flavour, and for ever afterwards they sang it that way when they played at Church.

Chapter Three

The Tree House

Lucy was lying in the hammock under the sycamore tree. One of her feet hung over the edge and with her toe she set the hammock gently swinging while she traced a pattern in the dust, for the children had swung there so often that there was a bald patch in the grass worn by their feet. Looking up into the heart of the sycamore she repeated over and over to herself words that she had heard for the first time that morning:

"To be carnally minded is death; but to be spiritually minded is life and peace."

"Carnally minded, carnally minded," she murmured. What proud, glowing words they were! She saw them as high-stepping, processional horses, caparisoned in scarlet. But why, if you were carnally minded, and it was wrong to be carnally minded, as was inferred, should the punishment be Death, since her mother had said that Death was something to be welcomed? When Nancy, the bay mare who had been stiff in her forelegs ever since Lucy could remember, was led away one day to be shot, the children were told that nothing but the worn-out husk was buried in the corner of the bottom hay-field; the real Nancy was no doubt galloping in heavenly pastures.

Then, if dying were of so little account, even something to be welcomed and treasured when it came, why did those words "To be carnally minded is Death" make her think of stepping into a cold room, from which the sun and the green waving trees and the gentle puffs of air that reached her from the garden and the heavy drone of bees over the flower-beds were barred out for ever?

"But to be spiritually minded is life"—that was easier to understand. Lucy wriggled round till she was seated in the hammock, dug her two feet into the dust and sent herself flying into the air. The green hill above the larch wood rose and sank; now she was like a bird darting straight into the sky; with each touch of her toe, each bend of her body, she was lifted high into a shining life. Even Nancy, though her legs were made young again in the meadows of God, would be no fleeter than Lucy, if only she might become spiritually minded!

Overhead the sycamore rustled its branches softly. Lucy was sure it liked her to swing there, for the sycamores were friendly trees. Not all the trees were friendly; some of them were jealous and lonely, like the circle of dark firs near the river. Often Lucy had set out to visit them, fearing their displeasure, for the wind never ceased sighing and thrumming through their branches.

The beeches were nicest of all. Delia and Lucy had each one of her own with secret holes in its trunk: wet mysterious holes where black rain-water collected, and dry holes where "conkers" were hoarded. Delia kept a valuable object in her tree a three-pronged fork that had once belonged to Beedles and with which he had often fried bacon over the saddle-room fire. She and Lucy used it for mixing their mud pies, but it was really Delia's fork.

The apple trees in the orchard were amusing, for they had grown old in the funniest ways, twisting themselves into shapes that resembled horses and ships and railway engines; yet somehow as trees they seemed less important than the others, except in the spring when they covered their gnarled branches with foaming blossom, and again in the autumn when the cider apples, that were so lovely to look at and so sour to taste, grew round and scarlet.

Chief of all the trees was the Tree House—a monster yew whose dark boughs, hung at morning with gleaming gossamers, stretched outside Delia's and Lucy's bedroom window. So thick were they that you might play beneath them in the rain without getting wet; on the hottest days they made a cool place of dim light, trodden earth and brown needles, where no grass ever grew and where the long, lean branches were polished smooth by the constant climbing and sliding of the children. Here were front stairs and back stairs, hall and kitchen, drawing-room and nurseries. Sometimes Delia and Lucy would bring out their dolls, their tea-sets and their tin baths, and then the bright beautiful day sped all too fast; no sooner, it seemed, was everything arranged to their satisfaction than it was time to go indoors to wash their hands for lunch, or to change their frocks because visitors were coming to tea; and when the trees were making long shadows across the lawn and the garden was more magical than ever, Louisa would tell them it was time to clear away all that "caudle," and everything must be carried once more up the stairs and down the long passage to the nursery and put tidily in its place.

Best of all perhaps were those days when, untrammelled by the dolls and their furniture (the table with its wooden flap which never stayed up, and the bath handle that was too stiff to turn), they simply "pretended"; when Lucy, no longer restrained by a toy piano of less than two octaves with a flat and wooden tone, could play divine sonatas up and down one of the branches, and converse with innumerable children, visitors and retainers, while Delia, who ruled in the kitchen, prepared exquisite meals of chopped leaves and petals.

Once from her airy perch in the branches Lucy looked down on Delia below, stirring a rich and liquid mud pie. At that moment she knew that she was completely happy and wished that she might for ever sit in a green tree-top with Delia just below, preparing imaginary feasts while she listened with sympathy and understanding to Lucy's conversation.

At night the trees seemed to creep round the house, and the blackbirds never ceased their flutings and their startled chuckles and chuggings among the bushes till the first stars came out over the hill. When at last they were silent the young owls hissed softly to each other on the beeches by the nursery window.

There was never such a place for birds. With the turn of the year the ploughed fields were white with gulls that bred near one of the mountain lakes; early in April the curlews came inland with their desolate cry which Delia's quick ears were always the first to catch, and the rooks clamoured and argued over their nests, breaking off twigs from the trees with a sideways wrench of their strong beaks, and walking mincingly on the lawn as they searched for moss.

Every year the house-martins built their nests outside Delia's and Lucy's bedroom window, and the drenched spring fields, where pools of rain-water winked with a thousand eyes, were full of tumbling, calling peewits. The pretty nut-hatches ran up and down the tree-trunks and the woodpeckers' rat-tat-tat echoed all day. They with their hammer and the great tits with their harsh sawing were as noisy as a carpenter's shop.

Along the river bank there were moor-hens, always engaged on some bustling business of their own, graceful dippers and water-wagtails, and the brilliant, shy kingfishers, while sometimes a heron stood pensively fishing, or winged his sulky flight to the remote and reedy haunts of the wild duck.

One morning something woke Lucy very early before it was quite light. While she lay still in bed one small, sleepy bird piped a note, another answered, and thereupon there burst out such a clamour of voices, such an urgency of song that this seemed to be no ordinary daybreak, but one made above all others for gladness and rejoicing. After that Lucy fell asleep and did not wake until Louisa came in to say it was past seven.

When Lucy told Delia about the birds she said they sang like that every morning—she had often heard them; nor was the day that followed in any way unusual. But Lucy never forgot the first time she heard them; she was certain it was a special morning. Perhaps, she reflected, no day was really ordinary; it was always meant to be new and exciting—if only one did not spoil it all.

Chapter Four

Queen Bertha

There was, at this time, so great a company of people inside the house, jostling each other on the stairs every evening, that sometimes it was not safe to go up and down alone. They were not noticeable to everyone, but Lucy knew all about them—their habits and peculiarities, and the tragedies of their lives, for they all had secret sorrows.

Perhaps the most unhappy, as well as the most beautiful, was the Innocent Child. This poor Creature was afflicted, quite undeservedly, by horrible pains and tortures: red-hot irons were thrust in and out of holes in her unresisting body; she was crushed slowly behind the doors of cupboards, shut up in chests of drawers for days and nights together and dragged over cobbles fastened to the tails of wild ponies: yet never a sigh nor a groan escaped her, so that she drew pity even from her torturers and heaped coals of fire on their heads.

"Have you heard what 'They' have done to the Innocent Child?" Lucy would ask in horror-laden tones. But she and Delia were not allowed to tell these tales to Miriam, who had a way of screaming in the night afterwards. There were also the Toothless Hag, who appeared when Lucy lost her first teeth, and—far more lasting and important—the Armenians.

It was their well-known afflictions that first endeared the Armenians to Lucy's tender heart. They took the stage early in the morning and complicated the business of dressing, which became, indeed, so long and intricate that there were times when even Lucy wished that all these odd creatures, who had taken so tenacious a hold on her life, could disappear for ever. Without them it might have been possible to accomplish her dressing with the same precision and speed as Delia, and to avoid those fierce encounters with Louisa which darkened the beginning of every day.

But the Armenians, having been summoned from the vasty deep, could not be so easily returned there. No sooner had Louisa carried in the large can of water every morning at seven o'clock than it instantly became a well outside the walls of a beleaguered city, while the wardrobe turned into the walls round which the gallant Greshenelie must climb at the peril of life and limb, returning triumphantly to the thirsting citizens with the brimming pitcher on her shoulder.

It was this same royal maid—a king's daughter and the idol of her people—who was so beset with unworthy suitors that she knew not which way to turn and finally dismissed them in the following song:

> "O, little lizards in the pond,
> I think you are of me more fond
> Than those who come to trouble me.
> O, little birds that sing and fly,
> I think for me you'd gladly die
> And would not stop to worry me."

Greshenelie composed her own music, and there are several pictures of her extant—drawn on the blank pages of old diaries—seated on the edge of a pond in pensive mood, with a posse of faint-hearted suitors in the background.

I have said that Greshenelie was of royal blood, but royalties were not uncommon in Delia's and Lucy's room. No sooner were they in bed than each of them became a reigning Queen. Delia was Catherine of England, and Lucy, as Bertha of France, was the mother of three fair sons who, in spite of their velvet jackets, might easily have been mistaken for toy monkeys by the uninitiated. George, the eldest, had a studious nature hidden by a rugged outside; Charles, a delicate creature, played the flute and said little. But Joseph, the youngest—ah, how shall I describe the gaiety and charm of Joseph, his mother's undisguised favourite, the wag of the Court, as you might guess at once from his merry upturned snout) No wonder that he played brilliantly on the violin, since his mother was a musician of note who performed with skill upon the rails of her bed, singing and accompanying songs of her own composition. "Oh, the green woods, oh, the sweet woods of France," was one of her loveliest lyrics; but she was also the author of a national song, sung at all State occasions:

> "Oh, the royal band of France
> Where you see the ladies dance
> On the royal, goyal fields
> Where the admiration deals!
>
> Oh, our good and gracious king
> Who makes the royal band to sing
> And makes the royal ladies bold
> To dance and play in chains of gold!"

"What does 'goyal' mean," asked Catherine of England.

"It's a French word," said her sister Queen carelessly. "I'm not sure of the English meaning."

It was a happy family, but even princes fade and lose their looks, and the lively Joseph, grown battered by his varied fortunes, lost an eye. Whereupon Louisa, being unusually amiable, took him away one evening and busied herself with needle and thread and some silver beads.

Now silver beads are all very well on a Christmas tree, but they should not replace the dark eyes of one's beloved. Any mother, waking at dawn to find her darling son beside her stating at her with the repellent eyes of a fish, should be excused if her feelings get the better of her. Louisa, coming in with the water, found a desolate, sobbing Queen Bertha on the bed, and Joseph lying on his back in a far corner of the room, surveying the ceiling and his unnatural fate with the bloodless gaze of philosophy.

All three brothers lived to an honourable old age and were buried together in the same grave, wrapped in a shroud of flannel. The tomb was inscribed with their names, a skull and cross-bones and the following epitaph:

> "A wild and chequered life was theirs
> Beneath the Blankets of a bed;
> Princes of noble fame, they now
> Lie proudly cold and dead."

Greshenelie and the thirsty Armenians were not the only delayers of dressing and undressing. There was also the Young Acrobat.

The Young Acrobat wore tights and would leap perilously from one piece of furniture to another, or hang suspended from a bed-rail above the quivering multitude that roared applause—hundreds of feet below. Among his friends were the Blue Lady and the White Lady, two sisters who lived in a feudal castle and could generally be seen at night, pacing the battlements and bewailing their lot. The White Lady was fond and foolish and deeply in love with the Young Acrobat, but the Blue Lady had a noble mind, a daughter and a passion for reciting aloud. She came to a sudden end by falling into the castle moat at the hottest moment of a siege.

Even the impassive Louisa was known to have been moved by the recital of her death, and Miriam sat up in bed spellbound. Lucy would begin in a thrilling voice: "She put her foot on the cold, marble step . . ."

"Don't go putting your bare feet on the washstand," Louisa interrupted.

"She looked at the great keep above her," the tragic tale

went on; "the rushing moat below. And all around she heard the sound of war and tumult. Then a voice cried: 'Mother! Mother' But she answered: 'Daughter! Daughter! What canst I do for thee?' "

"What canst she do?" asked Miriam, pausing with a spoonful of bread-and-milk half-way to her mouth.

"Don't interrupt," said Lucy. " 'What canst I do for thee?' 'Naught! naught! I will cast myself into the moat below.' "

"You'll break the springs of the bed if you go on like that," remarked Louisa, folding up the clothes.

Then Lucy thrust her head out of the bottom of the bed (where, by rights, her feet should have been) and cried dramatically:

"Thus ended the life of the beautiful Lady Mirabel!"

Louisa blew out the candle.

Chapter Five

The Hayfield

Early one June morning Delia jumped out of bed and ran to the window. "Lucy, quick, wake up!" she called, kneeling on the sill and craning her head out as far as it would go.

"Why? Where? What is it?" said Lucy, coming up from the bottom of the blankets where she slept curled up like a dormouse.

"It's the hay machine! You'll miss it in one moment."

But Lucy had already scrambled to the window, rubbing the sleep from her eyes. Coming up the drive, hidden every now and then by the trees, and looking enormous in the mist, was the hay-cutting machine. The clatter that it made on the stony drive grew nearer and nearer, and now Delia and Lucy could see the two big horses and the figure of a man perched on the little seat behind, as though he were riding on air.

"It's Denis! And he's brought Lofty and Stout!" screamed Delia and Lucy together, and they pranced about the room in their night-gowns, for they both loved Denis, and Lofty and Stout were their favourite names whenever they played horses—though neither of them liked being "Stout" and honourably took turns to be "Lofty."

Already Delia was pulling on her clothes, but Lucy knelt at the window and looked out into the garden. The dark needles of the Tree House were looped with grey cobwebs, and a missel-thrush, with plump, speckled breast, was hopping from branch to branch. The air was full of a soft twittering and the lawn below was grey with dew. Maurice's wooden cart and horse were lying under the sycamore where he had left them the evening before; they looked small and lonely and seemed, like everything else at this early hour, to be waiting for something to happen.

By the time Delia and Lucy were dressed the front door was open and Jane was scrubbing the step with a rasping sound. They ran round the house and through the stable-yard. Beedles was in the loose-box and called good-morning to them; Sam, the black retriever, saw them from his kennel and barked, asking to be let out; the pigs squealed at them from behind the woodpile, because they thought Beedles was bringing their breakfast, and the hens, who had met together to await their corn, scattered in indignation. The lane beyond the hayricks was dappled with sun, but the mist was still on the river. The water looked black and wicked, Lucy thought; not at all like the warm, bright river where they had bathed yesterday.

When they reached the hayfield, the white gate that led into it stood open. Davey John was there with his scythe, "opening up" the corners, and Denis, Lofty and Stout were far away. The clatter of the machine had turned to a gentle whirring, and whenever Denis came to the end of the row and backed the horses the whirr changed to a click-clack. He turned now and came towards Delia and Lucy, bouncing up and down on his seat and calling, "Come up, Lofty! Come up, my dear!", and the hay fell behind in long swathes—very cool and green at the roots.

" 'Morning, Miss Daylia. 'Morning, Miss Lucy," called Denis and showed his white teeth when he smiled. He pulled up the horses and Delia stroked their noses and patted their necks. But Lucy danced a dance all to herself in the middle of the green swathes while the sun grew hotter and sucked the mist from the river. Davey John was sharpening his scythe in the shadow of the hedge and Delia said suddenly: "I'm sure it's time for breakfast!"

*   *   *

Lessons that morning were dreadfully dull and tiresome. It was Miss Crabtree's day. She came on a bicycle three mornings a week to teach arithmetic, grammar and the Kings of England, so that there was no escaping these subjects for Delia and Lucy; whereas French and literature with their mother could be lightly postponed to make room for a picnic, and Latin with Mr. Vaughan, the Rector, had a way of disappearing altogether when he went away for a day's fishing, or to preach at a neighbouring harvest festival. But Miss Crabtree on her bicycle arrived with a horrid regularity, and to-day—of all days, with Denis in the hayfield—it was the turn for arithmetic.

Delia had begun vulgar fractions, but Lucy was still very shaky over long division, and she spent the whole lesson on a sum that sprawled down her page like the mouse's tail in "Alice in Wonderland." Her figures grew larger and more and more untidy, and she rubbed out one of them so often that there was a black hole in the middle of the page.

"Delia, you may go now," said Miss Crabtree. "Put your things tidily away. Lucy must remain until she has finished this sum to which she is not giving her attention."

Delia put her pencils by in their box with the picture of Lord Kitchener on the lid, and looked sadly at Lucy. Then she slipped out of the room, and Lucy heard the pad of her sand-shoes as she ran down the passage. Outside, the wood-pigeons were crooning, stopping suddenly in the middle of the sleepy sound: "Roo-roo, roo-roo. Roo-roo, roo-roo. Roo!" Perhaps they were saying: "Poor fool, poor fool. Poor fool, poor fool. Fool!" But it was all very well for wood-pigeons: they could sit in a tree all day without worrying over long division. Oh, why was it arithmetic to-day! Davey John had promised to make her a little wooden pitchfork to toss the hay; perhaps, by this time, Denis was giving Delia a ride on Lofty's back when the horses came up to have their midday bait in the stable. Soon the cutting would be finished and Denis would take

Lofty and Stout away with him; but she would miss it all—all because of a long-division sum!

She wouldn't cry, she wouldn't; and then suddenly a tear trickled down her nose and splashed on to the black hole in the paper; she seized her piece of india-rubber and scrubbed: the hole grew enormous, with damp and flabby edges, and Miss Crabtree said coldly: "If you would only think for a moment, Lucy, instead of rubbing out what you have already written, you would soon finish that sum."

But Lucy knew it was no use trying to think. The inside of her mind was black, black as the hole in the paper, and her tears ran down so fast that it was no use trying to stop them.

Then suddenly the lovely thing happened: below the school-room window her father's voice called: "Hullo, you in there! Who's coming down to the hayfield,"

Miss Crabtree rose and went quickly to the window. "Delia has gone already, Mr. Gwyn," she said. "I am sorry to say that Lucy has not yet finished her arithmetic."

"Pity to stay indoors on a morning like this," came the answer, and Lucy held her breath. Then she heard her father whistle to the dogs, and his footsteps died away. Miss Crabtree came back to the table.

"As your father seems anxious that you should be out of doors, Lucy, you may leave that sum," she said. "But understand that this must not happen again.

Next time you must give your attention to what you are doing."

What cared Lucy for next time! She flung her books higgledy-piggledy on to the shelf and raced down the stairs. The dairy door was open and inside Jane was churning with a splodgy sound. Lucy all but knocked over a bucket of water as she rushed past. "For pity's sake, look where you're going!" she heard Jane's voice call after her as she ran out into the sunshine. The hens were sitting drowsily in the hay-bay, and the river had lost its cold mist and dark looks of early morning. The hot sun shone on her head and the stones in the lane felt sharp beneath her sand-shoes, but she ran all the way without stopping. When she reached the white gate, she saw Delia in the corner under the oak trees, watching Denis unharness Lofty and Stout; and when Denis saw Lucy he lifted her up on to Lofty's back so that she rode proudly out of the field.

"Did you finish that sum?" asked Delia. "I thought Crab-apple would keep you there all the morning " But Lucy only laughed and shouted, digging her bare knees into Lofty's warm flanks, and Denis called: "Woa, horsel Come up, Lofty, my dear!"

*   *   *

Two days later everyone was in the hayfield—raking the hay into windrows and gathering the windrows into cocks. The men walked in line: the children's father, Beedles, Jarman, Davey John and Twm the Weeg. Twm was Mr. Gwyn's gamekeeper. He was a splendid man who carried ferrets about in bags, could tcll you stories of polecats and discover the secret springs of water with nothing more than a peeled stick. The Weeg, where he lived, was away beyond the Long Moel where Lucy had never been, though Delia had sometimes ridden there on the pony with her father. Twm's face was round and red, like the sun on a frosty evening. Looking one day at Jarman's yellow skin and black hair, Lucy had asked him why his face was so different from Twm's.

"Twm's hot from walking, seemingly. The Weeg's a tidy way off," Jarman answered rather crossly, and Lucy wished that she could have been at the Weeg early in the morning to see Twm's face before he set out to walk over the Long Moel.

To-day it was redder than ever, for the sun poured down all day on the hayfield, and the men worked with their shirts open on their chests. In the shade of the oak trees by the hedge stood the great cans of cider and the blue-and-white hooped mugs. There was tea in the hayfield for everyone: the maids carried it down from the house in big baskets and spread the white cloths on the cropped grass.

Towards evening, when the children's mother had left the field, Louisa sat in the middle of the biggest cock with Miriam asleep in her lap while Maurice ran about burying himself and calling to the others to find him. Delia worked steadily, walking behind the men and raking tidily round the cocks. So too did Lucy— for a time. But soon she grew tired; the rough handle of the rake blistered her hand; she moved too quickly so that sometimes she rnissed the hay altogether, and then the teeth of her rake would become embedded in the ground or entangled in the buttercup runners. At last she flung the rake away and ran over to Delia.

"List thou to me!" she said. It was their secret way of saying "I have an idea"; and Delia answered: "My ears are opened." Only they did not say this in their ordinary voices, but half-sang it, as people do in church.

"Let's go and paddle in the brook," said Lucy in her ordinary voice.

"But we aren't allowed to go there alone," Delia objected. "And Louisa won't bring Maurice and Miriam because it's nearly their bed-time."

"Well, I won't paddle then," said Lucy. "But I'll go and make ducks and drakes. I'm tired of raking."

She ran across the field to the corner under the oak trees where, a month ago, the bluebells had made a purple mist in the grass, crawled through the fence and slid down the bank. The brook joined the river here and on the strip of gravelly sand were many smooth, flat pebbles, made on purpose, it seemed, for "ducks and drakes." Lucy soon found as many as she could carry, but she could never make her "ducks and drakes" hop more than twice, whereas Delia, had she been there, would have sent them skimming across the stream.

Lucy grew tired of trying and sat down to consider the opposite bank. It looked much more exciting over there; the trees were twisted into curious shapes and their roots hung in pink tassels down to the water. Suddenly she saw two bright eyes watching her, and then what she had thought to be a piece of brown mud moved quickly along the water's edge and Lucy saw four little feet scurrying and a little nose twitching. She said "Oh!" very softly, and the rat looked at her and slipped into a hole.

A kingfisher flew suddenly out of the bushes close to where the rat had disappeared; the sun shone a moment on its pink breast before it was gone, curtseying and skimming, drawing blue loops from bank to bank. Perhaps it had left a nest somewhere near. Lucy remembered one that her father had shown her—a round hole in the bank, smelling of fish. What a fine thing that would be to show Delia, if she could only find it! Off came her sand-shoes, which were hot and full of tickly pieces of hay; the water curled deliciously round her toes; it was warm at the edges, but in the middle it rushed coldly past her bare ankles. She wondered whether she ought not really to go back; she thought she heard Louisa's voice calling, and with that she ran splashing through the water and scrambled up the bank, her toes sinking in the soft mud.

The other side of the brook was as different as could be; the grass was soft under Lucy's feet and the field stretched into the distance so that it seemed that there was nothing between her and the blue hills: a cuckoo called its broken June note and a rabbit looked at Lucy and popped into its hole. It seemed silly to bother about the kingfisher's nest when there was a whole new field to play in. What a pity Delia and Maurice had not come too! And then, just as she was thinking she would like someone to talk to, Ned Lovell stepped out of the bushes.

Ned Lovell was half-gipsy and the best fisherman in the countryside. He had twinkling brown eyes dlat matched his brown velvet jacket. When he saw Lucy he called out: "A fine evening, m'dear. The fish are rising nicely."

"Have you caught any," asked Lucy, and at that he showed her his basket, with three shining, speckled fish inside.

"If you'll come along with me I'll be showing you how to catch a trout."

"Then I'll come," said Lucy, and she skipped by Ned's side, showed him the blister on her hand and told him about the water-rat, the long-division sum and Miss Crabtree.

"No use whatever in book-larnin'," said Ned Lovell. "No one ever learnt nothing from old books. You listen to what the river says, my little dear, and watch Ned catch a trout for supper."

He showed her how to fasten a fly on the line, and Lucy sat on the bank and watched him cast upstream so that the current caught the line and brought it gently down. A little breeze sprang up to ripple the water, and Ned's shadow with its moving arm and dhe shadows of the willows grew longer and longer in the sunny field. Just below them a big fish jumped "Splosh," leaving wide circles.

"Did 'ee see that one?" Ned whispered excitedly. "It was a fair monsterl"

Suddenly the line tightened and ran out with a scream of the reel, and there was a fish struggling at the end of it. Lucy nearly shouted with excitement, for just as it seemed that Ned had made sure of the fish it darted away, and when at last it was landed Ned seized her by the shoulder and whispered: "Couch down! Couch down!" Together they crouched behind the bushes while Ned took the leaping fish off the hook.

"Why did we have to hide?" asked Lucy when the fish was lying still in the basket.

"Well now," said Ned, "it wouldn't do to be ashowing of ourselves, but you come along with me and I'll tell you all there is to know about catching a trout."

"I'd like to come with you very much," said Lucy politely,

"but I think perhaps I ought to be getting back. You see, I go to bed at half-past six. Maurice goes at six and Delia's started to stay up till seven just a little time ago."

"The light's good," said Ned, "and the fish is rising nicely."

"But you don't know Louisa when she's cross," Lucy objected. At that Ned sat down on the bank, took out a clay pipe and appeared to ponder the matter.

"No, I don't know Louisa," he said at last, lighting his pipe and puffing slowly. "But I tell you what way it is I've allus found women; leastways the women I've had to deal with, and they're seemingly alike."

But Lucy never heard what Ned thought of women, for at that moment she heard her name being called, and at that sound of doom she stood up and held out her hand to Ned.

"Good-bye," she said. "It's very kind of you to have let me come with you. But you see it is Louisa, and there's no two ways about it." This was a favourite remark of Louisa's own and seemed suited to the gravity of the occasion.

Around her stretched the delectable meadow. It was full of rabbits now. They had all come out to feed, big ones and little ones, sitting upright above their front doors into which they popped at sight of Lucy. A golden mist of late sunlight lay everywhere and the air was full of the bleating of sheep and the breath of hay borne across the stream. Behind her lay adventure, fresh playing-fields and the heady companionship of Ned Lovell; in front lay retribution—Louisa and dry bread for supper. With a sigh Lucy made her way back, slid down the bank and stepped reluctantly into the water. It felt much colder now, and where exactly, she wondered, half-way across, had she left her shoes?

*   *   *

Lucy did not see Ned Lovell again for a long time, but after that day she and Maurice had a new game. They would make fishing-rods with sticks and pieces of string, and whenever one of them pretended to catch a fish the other would call out: "Did 'ee see that one? It's a fair monster! Couch down, there, couch down!"

Chapter Six

Sunday

On Sunday mornings Delia and Lucy wore starched, frilly pinafores instead of their everyday holland overalls, and breakfasted downstairs with their father and mother. There were sausages in a brown dish, honey in the comb, and a feeling of peace and expectation in the air, as though something exciting—but nothing in the least wicked—might happen at any moment.

After breakfast was over Delia would carry from its shelf the heavy, large-print Bible and lay it open on the nursery table. For some time now she and Lucy had been learning by heart the 103rd Psalm—the one that has the splendid verse about the eagle: "Who satisfieth thy mouth with good things: so that thy youth is renewed like the eagle's."

Further on there is one that smells like a hayfield: "As for man, his days are as grass; as a flower of the field, so he flourisheth. For the wind passeth over it and it is gone; and the place thereof shall know it no more."

But before Lucy could reach that part there were many hard and nobbly verses that seemed made to torment her. However many times she read from the page before her: "He hath not dealt with us after our sins; nor rewarded us according to our iniquities," she could not repeat the words without the book, nor remember what came afterwards. Delia, meanwhile, had sailed triumphantly to the end: "Bless ye the Lord, all ye His hosts; ye ministers of His, that do His pleasure. Bless the Lord, all His works in all places of His dominion."

Lucy imagined the "dominion" as some vague colony where the inhabitants wore sailor hats—possibly because she and Delia possessed sailor hats with "H.M.S. Dominion" embroidered on the ribbons; but the "ministers" were quite plain to her—hurrying to and fro in black clerical coats. To-day they seemed very small and far away. Just outside the window the rooks were cawing and quarrelling in the beech trees, and she could hear Maurice's voice as he played in the garden. Lucy fidgeted in her chair, fingering the blue satin book-marker, whereon a great-aunt of hers had stitched the words: "Open Thou mine eyes, that I may behold wondrous things out of Thy law."

"You're not learning properly," said Delia.

It was a relief when Louisa bustled in to say it was time to get ready for church, and the great Bible was put away for another week. To go to church Delia and Lucy wore white serge coats and Leghorn hats with white satin bows; Lucy's hat had a new piece of elastic which was too tight and made a pink mark under her chin—but Louisa had no patience with such vagaries. Downstairs the front door stood open and the children's father was outside with the dogs leaping round him— old Sam, the curly, black retriever; Bell and Juno, the two setters, lean and trembling with excitement, and Jenny, the rough-haired terrier, who liked coming to church but preferred a rat-hunt. Beedles, wearing his shirt-sleeves and walking stiffly because of the rheumatics in his legs, came round to the front door, wheeling Mr. Gwyn's bicycle; the dogs grew demented with excitement.

"I'm going on. Someone give Matthew a drink of cider when he brings the letters," said the children's father. Then he jumped on his bicycle and rode down the drive under the green lime-flowers, with the dogs streaming behind him.

Delia and Lucy and their mother drove to church in a low phaeton, drawn by Taffy, the chestnut pony. Mrs. Gwyn now came out of the house, wearing a hat trimmed with feathers and a black ribbon round her white throat. Running after her came Sarah, the parlour-maid, with the blue velvet prayer-book bag which had nearly been left behind.

"Don't forget to pull down the sun-blinds," Mrs. Gwyn called. She said this every Sunday, and Sarah always answered: "I won't, ma'am." It was the signal for Taffy to start, which he did "like a shot out of a gun," as Beedles remarked, for he was a hill pony and would follow the hounds, on a hunting day, till he dropped. The phaeton had belonged to Mr. Gwyn's mother in the days before rubber tyres were known; it made a noise that was something between a threshing-machine and cavalry going into action.

The road wound through the valley between banks that were misty with cow-parsley, and Mrs. Gwyn unfurled her sunshade while Taffy slowed to a walk on the hill. They met no one on their way, excepting Matthew, walking with the friend whom he always called his "Butty." Matthew was a gentle, white-haired man who brought the Pengarth letters every Sunday. His companion was sad and dark-eyed, and no one knew his name; he was simply "Matthew's Butty."

Outside the church the Rector waited a little anxiously: his hay was still out and there was certainly a feeling of thunder in the air; the leaves of the poplars in the churchyard fluttered pale green against a darkening sky. He hoped the threat of rain would not keep the Gwyn family at home, because there were so few people to preach to on Sunday morning—only his own family; Jarman, the gardener from Pengarth, with his daughter Kate; old Ann Elias who wasn't quite right in the head, and the Rectory garden-boy who cleaned the boots and knives and was the only candidate for confirmation. So the Reverend Daniel Vaughan was very glad when he saw Mr. Gwyn with Bell, Juno, Sam and Jenny, and heard, behind them, the distant roar of the phaeton.

"They're coming, my dear," he called over the hedge to his wife, and hurried into church.

The inside of Pengarth Church reminded Lucy of the potato-house at home: they both had the same cool, earthy smell. Kneeling on a hassock that scratched her bare knees she peeped between her fingers at the disciples in the East window with their curly beards and red dressing-gowns. Glancing round at the bent heads of the congregation she wondered excitedly whether, as God was in the midst of them, she might surprise Him by suddenly lifting the green curtain on the chancel wall. When she sat back in the pew Lucy could stretch down her toes and touch the rough, hairy back of Jenny the terrier, who lay in the bottom of the pew all through the service while the other dogs were fastened into the Rectory stable. Jenny was very quiet—much quieter than Lucy; only her rubbery nose, which she kept close to her master's feet, never ceased movmg.

Mr. Vaughan, whose delight was in music, played the harmonium himself, drawing from its wheezy body a great sweetness of sound. The hymns were not arranged beforehand; he chose them as he pleased in the course of the service, turning over and over the pages of a tattered hymn-book, during which time Mr. Gwyn read the lessons in a pleasant, hurried voice, as though he apologised to his listeners for keeping them so long. In the middle of the last hymn the Rector left the harmonium and advanced to the altar. The unaccompanied singing that followed always filled Lucy with misgiving: her parents' voices, Mrs.

Vaughan's shrill notes and the cracked cackle from Ann Elias in the pew behind sounded so forlorn.

On this Sunday morning the church grew darker until even the red gowns of the apostles glowed dimly and Mr. Vaughan, thinking of his hay, looked up anxiously. Through the clear glass of the side window Lucy could see the tall grass round the tombstones waving frantically in a sudden wind, and the leaves of the poplar whipped till they showed their silver backs. She pulled Delia's sleeve to draw her attention to these exciting things that were going on outside, but Delia was following the Prayer for the King very intently in her new green leather Prayer Book and frowned at Lucy.

After that Lucy wriggled round in her seat so that she could see the Rectory pew. Lena, wearing her pink hat, had her face buried in her hands; Peggy and Olwen, with their heads together, were whispering, and David openly made a face at Lucy. It was one of his worst faces and the wickedness of making it in church so appalled even Lucy that she could not think of a suitable one in return and turned her back on him instead. Then, quite suddenly, in the middle of the second lesson, an enormous clap of thunder broke over the church. The Rector, who was searching for a hymn, jumped in his chair; Mr. Gwyn looked up quickly and then went on reading:

"What thou seest, write in a book, and send it unto the seven churches which are in Asia; unto Ephesus, and unto Smyrna, and unto Pergamos, and unto Thyatira, and unto Sardis, and unto Philadelphia, and unto Laodicea . . ."

No thunderstorm ever seemed so terrific to Lucy as the one which broke over Pengarth that Sunday. Every minute the church seemed to grow larger and darker and she herself smaller and colder. The thunder crashed and rattled overhead, completely muffling the sound of Jarman counting the collection money in the vestry. Lucy decided that God was no longer hiding behind the green curtains: He must be flinging the clouds across the sky. Outside, the rain fell in arrowy streams and the gutters on the church roof gushed waterfalls. By the end of the service there was a great puddle before the porch, and they all ran for shelter to the Rectory by the little path between the gravestones and the border of drenched pinks.

"I'm sorry for that hay of yours, Vaughan," said Mr. Gwyn. The Rector was wiping the rain from his hat with his pocket-handkerchief.

"Yes," he said, "you were wise to cut yours so early —but you always were a lucky man."

While they stood talking in the little dark drawing-room Mrs. Vaughan was running up and downstairs carrying cloaks and bonnets, and at last they drove home through the rain wrapped in strange clothes and sheltered by the Rector's big umbrella. Lucy had an ugly brown cape with bone buttons belonging to Olwen, but Delia wore Lena's scarlet hood for which Lucy secretly longed. Their Leghorn hats were put into a cardboard box of Mrs. Vaughan's, and placed at the bottom of the phaeton. The pony, having its head towards home, went more than ever "like a shot out of a gun," and the dogs, freed at last from the Rectory stable, rushed on ahead. All the way, on either side of the road, were streams of bright brown water, and the meadow-sweet on the banks hung heavily.

That day was memorable in the annals of the Gwyn family, because from that time onwards a large cardboard box was carried to church in the bottom of the phaeton to hold Delia's and Lucy's hats in case of rain. It was called the "Sunday Box."

Chapter Seven

They go a Journey

Aunt Shân—but even the children called her Shân— lived in a house by the sea. Great were the preparations when the family went to stay with her: Delia, Lucy and Maurice were so excited at thought of the journey that, when at last the day came, they could eat neither breakfast nor lunch. Lunch, which had to be eaten at twelve o'clock, was particularly difficult; it was almost impossible to swallow rice-pudding while the men, in their heavy boots, were clumping upstairs to carry down the boxes.

The railway company obligingly allowed the midday train to stop at Pengarth Halt whenever the children's father wished to take his family to the sea, which was very convenient for everyone except Beedles and Jarman, who had to carry all the trunks through the rick-yard and down the leafy lane, and bump them over the bridge across the river as far as Mrs. Bound's station platform, where she had set out a row of chairs among the sunflowers and sweet-peas. Such a lot of luggage! As well as the black trunks, shaped like Noah's ark, there were Miriam's perambulator and Louisa's sewing-machine, Delia's and Lucy's and Maurice's spades and buckets and several hampers full of vegetables from the garden. There were also a yellow tin bath, with a lid on top, and the "board"—two planks, fastened together and planed by Pugh the carpenter, on which Delia and Lucy lay down in turn for half-an-hour every afternoon, in the hope that they might cease to be round-shouldered.

The only dog they were allowed to take was Jenny the fox-terrier, for Shân did not care for dogs as well as children running all over her house, but Delia brought with her Jack

Baba, the old black-and-white rabbit, fastened in a basket. Lucy was responsible for nothing except her dolls. She decided to take Mabel, who had never been to the sea, and of course George, Charles and Joseph, who had been almost as many times as Lucy herself. She packed all their clothes in the yellow dolls' trunk—the three monkeys' velvet capes and Mabel's night-gown and silk bonnet and little red shoes. How was it, then, that in the bustle and excitement of departure, when everyone else had so much to think of, Lucy came to forget the yellow trunk? She remembered it only when they were all assembled on the station platform, and the colours of the day, that had been so fair a moment since, were suddenly blotted out. She told Delia, for it was impossible to keep such a gnawing sorrow to oneself, and Delia told Louisa. Soon everyone knew, and Lucy stood with burning cheeks while her mother said sadly:

"And that was all you had to remember, Lucy."

"Send Jarman back to fetch the thing, whatever it is," said the children's father. "There's still time."

Oh, words of comfortable hope! Jarman is the fastest walker in the parish—a long scissors of a man. He sets off at once, and immediately it seems that everyone else has forgotten the matter. Louisa and Bessie, the housemaid, are counting the boxes; Maurice is clamouring to be given his spade and bucket already; their mother is giving last instructions to Beedles and their father is chatting with Mrs. Bound. Only Lucy watches the lane in agony of mind, and strains her ears for the sound of the train. Suppose it comes now, and poor Jarman has run all that way for nothing! Is that the train? No, only the engine at the stone quarry. Then at last she sees him—good old Jarman, running at a long, loping trot, like a collie-dog, with the little yellow trunk safely under his arm. Dear, kind Jarman! Now everything has come right again—at least for a time.

The journey down to the sea is varied and thrilling,

beginning with the excitement of seeing their own hayfields and kitchen garden from the train. Then comes Mr. Williams's farm-house, with a perfectly new view of his duckpond and the red-and-white heifers standing in the yard. Now they are passing Pengarth Church and Rectory, and there is Mary Ellen, the Rectory maid, standing at the back door, and the gravestones in the churchyard looking different from usual. Beyond the Rectory the river winds its unexplored way, caressing new, untrodden strips of shingle where no one ever makes "ducks and drakes", curving past reedy corners where they catch sight of a lonely heron or a sudden flight of duck. And now they have reached the next station—a junction islanded in fields —where the porters shout "Change here for South Wales!", and there actually is a train waiting to go to South Wales—that unknown country—and people strolling unconcernedly to catch it. Then on and up, the engine chugging slowly into the hills where bog cotton grows at the side of the line, and a buzzard beats its wings against the sky, and so down through steep valleys where the little patchwork fields climb up to meet the bracken, and all the chattering streams come running with the children to the sea.

Miriam had fallen asleep on Louisa's lap; Delia was reading "What Katy Did," and Lucy and Maurice played trains. Maurice was the engine-driver and ticket-collector and Lucy was the passenger with a great many babies and bundles.... They made such a noise that they woke Miriam, and Louisa was cross.

After that Lucy made up a poem about some cattle-trucks, a station-master, a guard and three porters. She recited it aloud to the others; Maurice and Miriam liked it especially. This was the poem:

THE CATTLE TRUCKS

Look at those cattle trucks going down a hill!
Surely at the bottom they'll have a nasty spill!
Just at the bottom, under a tree,
Upset the cattle-trucks, one, two, three.

 Along came the station-master, hat all a-jug,
Picked up a beetle, picked up a slug;
Squashed them in his fingers, one, two, three,
Looked at the cattle-trucks under the tree.

Then he fetched a rope and he pulled very hard
And he called "Yo ho" to the lazy old guard;
Along came the porters, one, two, three,
Stared at the cattle trucks under the tree.

Then they got some string and a thick
    piece of twine
And soon pulled the cattle-trucks on to the line.
Away went they all from under the tree,
Away went the cattle-trucks, one, two, three.

"What does 'a-jug' mean," asked Delia.

Lucy said she could not explain exactly, but it was something old and just a little bit crooked.

During the last part of the journey the train rushes through tunnels, and between each tunnel there is the sea—miles of shining estuary, stretching to the blue hills.

"Look, look, the tide is in!" the children cry, crowding to the window. It is lucky, they feel, when the tide is in, and the little waves lap the shore. Then another tunnel swallows them, and Maurice knocks his spade on the floor and cries in the darkness "Listen! There's Davey Morris digging potatoes!", for everyone knows that the last tunnel of all runs under

Shân's garden, and soon, quite soon they will be there, and, because they have come a journey, Shân will be asking them all if they would like an egg with their tea.

*   *   *

Shân's house was as different from home as any house could well be, for it stood in the middle of the village, with only the street between it and the water, so that after you had gone to bed you could hear the swish and slap of the waves, and the noise of people walking to and fro and talking in Welsh. Delia and Lucy—sharing the feather bed in Shân's top bedroom with a bolster between to keep them from kicking each other—listened in awe to those flapping feet, those throats that seemed in such constant need of clearing. After the silence of home, the soft owl noises and gentle murmur of the river to which they were used, these sounds assumed enormous proportions. That first night, when they were still too excited to sleep, they lay and listened to the feet, wondering from which direction they came—for it is impossible to tell this when you are lying in bed—and why so many people should be walking about outside, when all the children should have been in bed, and all the grown-ups talking in their drawing-rooms.

Waking early next morning Lucy watched the pale light creep like the rising tide round each familiar object in the room—the ghostly mirror with its gilt top, the steep, cliff side of the vast mahogany wardrobe, the unchanging ornaments on the mantelpiece. She slipped out of bed, and stood barefoot and entranced, watching the morning tide brim the wide estuary, while the sun rose behind the waiting hills. Then silver turned to gold and a pathway of vivid fire ran straight from the far shore to Shân's house, and Lucy longed, with an almost unbearable longing, to step into a little boat, which she would keep moored outside the front door. Then she would row along that shining track into the world where nothing stirred, unless it were a cormorant, with neck outstretched, or the gulls rocking gently on the water.

Chilled to the bone, she ran back to bed, and stretching her toes round the bottom of the bolster touched Delia's warm foot.

"Delia, are you awake? Let's play Queen Bertha!"

"Very well. But you must keep your side of the bolster."

"I can't. It doesn't go to the bottom."

"But you're stretching your toes round the corner."

"No, I'm not. At least, not now. Do play."

"Oh, all right. What have you been doing to-day, my dear?"

It was Delia's voice no longer, but the voice of Catherine of England, addressing her sister sovereign of France, and at that—her favourite cue—Queen Bertha curled herself comfortably against the broad-backed bolster and began a narrative of exploits, unfettered by circumstance, until such time as Louisa entered, with a summons to rise which even queens must obey.

Chapter Eight

The House by the Sea

Part I

Shân's house stood where sea and river met. Over the water you looked to delectable islands of yellow sand where no children ever built castles or filled their buckets, for at high tide these islands disappeared beneath the waves. Beyond them lay a streak of green bog where a train—looking no bigger than Maurice's toy engine—wound its way; and between the bog and the sand-hills were little white houses, where, it was to be supposed, children stood at their nursery windows, looking over the water to Shan's house, just as Lucy stood looking at them.

In between the two shores ran John Knocker's ferryboat—the "Fairy Boat," Miriam called it. The children would stand at their window on blowy days, watching the little craft beat like a gull against the wind. When at last she touched the further shore the small black figures of the passengers would move away—slowly, slowly as flies crawling on a window-pane—till yellow sands, green bog and blue hills swallowed them up. Or, another day, it was the black speck that appeared first on the further shore and, gradually approaching, would resolve itself into several specks, waving their arms until such time as John Knocker and his boat answered the signal. These things could all be seen from Shân's drawing room window, through the snapdragons in the window boxes and the leaves of the magnolia tree; they could be seen better from Shân's bedroom, when you slipped in to play with her silver brushes and glass scent-bottles; better still from the nursery at the top of the house, and best of all from the garden. For Shân was

supremely lucky; instead of walking out of her door like
anyone else when she visited her garden, hers was the fun of
walking upstairs past her own bedroom, of crossing a bridge
that hung suspended over her backyard, and then climbing yet
more steps, where grown-ups paused to pant. And what an
amusing garden it was—so different from the lawns and
orchards, the hidden places and green silences of home. For
here were tiny paths, where two could not walk abreast,
running between bushes of fuchsia, valerian ant veronica, and
great blowsy hydrangeas that sprawled across the stone steps.
When you sat in the summer-house, half-way up, you saw the
blue water between the apple-boughs—little, stunted trees
where the apples grew so round and heavy that they never
waited to be picked, but dropped off themselves and went
rolling down among the tangled flowers, the shining cobwebs
and droning bees. If Jane, the cook, stood at the bottom with a
pie-dish in her hand she might catch them, thought Lucy. But
Shân told the children to pick them up, and they would fill
their pinafores with them as they ran before her, when she
advanced with determination, key in hand, up the garden path.

Through the garden door they stepped into a different
world. For here, on the hill, lived the Poet, and the Vicar's
donkey—very old and bad-tempered and tethered to a post
among the gorse bushes. Here too lived Perceval Tudor, with
his mother and French governess, and Mrs. Hughes-Jenkins,
who once gave Lucy a slice of seed-cake when Shân took her
there on a morning call. The room was full of china
ornaments, and there was a musical box which played "The
Minstrel Boy." All the time Shân and Mrs. Hughes-Jenkins
were talking Lucy was pulling the seeds out of her cake. She
felt it would be rude not to eat the cake, but it was difficult to
avoid the seeds, which she disliked. Soon there was a
monstrous pile of crumbs on her plate, and Mrs. Hughes-
Jenkins said tartly:

"That child doesn't like her cake. She should have said so before."

Shân made excuses, but Lucy was covered with shame, and for years she hated the tune of "The Minstrel Boy" as much as the taste of seeds.

Further up the hill—but not so far as the Poet— lived Mr. Powell, who liked girls better than boys, and would sometimes ask Delia and Lucy to tea. Mr. Powell knew exactly how to conduct a tea-party. Instead of wasting time sitting on chairs he took one straight to a room where the best toys were laid out on the floor—a fishing-pond with rods and magnets, and a farm-yard stocked with animals, trees and gates that opened and shut. Lucy, in particular, had reason to be grateful to Mr. Powell, as you may now hear.

At Easter time the window of the sweet-shop in the village was filled with chocolate eggs, fish and yellow chickens. In the front of the window was a cradle with a pink bow on top and two chocolate babies inside. Every day when Lucy went on the daily walk with Louisa, her eyes rested lovingly on those babies. She did not want to eat them, but simply to possess them, to take them in and out of that pink cradle, to hold them in her hands and rock them to sleep. Each morning, when they passed the shop, Louisa scolded her for loitering. As Easter Day drew near, Lucy grew terrified lest someone should buy the cradle and she never more see her chocolate babies. She even prayed that this would not happen and then—noting the success of the manoeuvre—prayed that Louisa would be moved to choose that direction for their walk. This was not unlikely, since Louisa's friend, Mair, the coalman's daughter, lived near the sweet-shop.

One morning, when Delia and Maurice had stayed at home with colds in their heads, Louisa and Lucy saw Mair standing at her door in a blue dress, with her red hair blowing in the wind. Louisa stopped pushing the pram and began to talk, and

Lucy hung behind and pressed her face against the window. The chocolate babies were now so familiar to her that she knew they were not exactly alike. One of them had a blotched eye and was a trifle smaller than his brother, and this one, because he looked sad, Lucy loved the better.

"Well," said a voice behind her, "what are you gazing at so hard," It was Mr. Powell. "Come in with me and choose something," he said, and before Lucy could reply, he had led her into the shop, where Mrs. Jones the Sweets reigned over her glass jars of barley-sugar and bull's-eye peppermints.

"Now then, which is it to be," said Mr. Powell genially. "I think I can guess," he added, for Lucy was still speechless.

"I believe it's that chicken in an egg she's set her heart on; don't you, Mrs. Jones? Will you get it down for us,"

Mrs. Jones was generally a slow-moving woman, but with the most unnatural alacrity she lifted the miserable chicken in its chocolate egg from the shelf and carefully blew the dust off it. She was wrapping it up in paper and Mr. Powell had his hand in his pocket when at last Lucy found words. She heard her own voice say, loudly and abruptly: "I don't want that one!", and immediately she was abashed and horrified at her rudeness. Her eyes filled with tears; the joy which had been so great, a moment since, turned to misery even more acute.

"Tut, tut," said Mr. Powell, a little put out, while Mrs. Jones stopped in the middle of making up the parcel.

"Well, which is it you want then?"

So the goal was once more in sight; the babies might yet be hers. With her finger she pointed them out, and Mrs. Jones had to climb on to the counter, her stays and shoes creaking, before she could reach the pink cradle. At last it was tied in a parcel, Mr. Powell laid the money on the counter and they stood in the street once more.

"Well, young lady, it's well to know your own mind. Give my respects to your aunt." With that he was gone, and Lucy ran after Louisa, hugging her parcel to her breast. And yet (so do the gods cheat us of our joy), the precious object, now at last her possession, no longer cradled unalloyed delight. Probably, she reflected, it had cost a great deal more money than the chicken, and she had heard her aunt sometimes talk of "Poor Mr. Powell." How ungraciously she had refused his first offer; how inadequately just because she wanted it so badly—she had thanked him for his present! She hoped to see him again and tell him that she loved it, but soon after this, when Maurice had eaten one-and-a-half of the babies and Louisa had thrown away the rest, she heard Shân say that Mr. Powell had sold his house and gone away to a foreign country.

*　　*　　*

Next door to Mrs. Jones the Sweets was Mrs. Roberts the Paper-shop, and both Delia and Lucy were pleased whenever Shân sent them there to buy a ball of string or a packet of labels. Mrs. Roberts had dark bright eyes and the prettiest, softest voice, and she never forgot anyone's face, nor what they would be likely to want. On wet summer days, when the shop was full of English visitors in dripping mackintoshes hunting for postcards, Mrs. Roberts knew exactly which of them would want a view of the Happy Valley, and which of them fancied a funny one of a golfer or a goat or a lady in a Welsh hat. She would explain to Colonel Frazer why his copy of The Times had not come, while handing Mr. Jenkins the Western Mail, and she would bend down to talk softly in Welsh to the children who toddled in, clasping their pennies to buy a bucket or a coloured balloon. When Delia or Lucy came she appeared to be delighted:

"There's nice to see you again, cariad! Shopping for Auntie, are you? Well, well, there's useful you are, to be sure!"

Lucy made up her mind to keep a shop like Mrs. Roberts's when she grew up. Everyone would be so pleased to buy things from her, and in between times she could always be reading a book behind the counter.

The Poet, chiefest of their friends, lived a long way up the hill behind Shân's house; so far that the children grew tired long before they reached the top and wished their legs were longer. The Poet said it was an unkind creature called Gravity that pulled them back; if it were not for Gravity—whom Maurice fancied as a long-armed monster lurking at the bottom—they would all shoot up the hill like corks out of a bottle. Near the top of the hill a grassy lane ran to the Poet's garden door. It was no use going there in the middle of the afternoon because that was the time of day when the Poet got up, so that when he asked you to tea it was really his breakfast, and no doubt he sat down to his lunch just as Delia and Lucy were being hauled off to bed.

There were other ways, besides the ordering of time, in which the Poet's house differed from those which the children visited with Shân. These other houses all had "silver tables" in their drawing-rooms; shelves covered with china, walls hung with samplers and water-colours. Books stood, untouched and unchanging, on their book-shelves, except for a few which, like little girls in their party-frocks, lay for inspection on small tables.

The same ones had lain on Shân's table ever since Lucy could remember—two bound volumes of the "Ladies' Magazine"; Dickens's "Christmas Carol"; "Tristan and Iseult" in green suede, and "Scenes from Clerical Life." Their positions were never altered. Shân, wearing a little muslin apron, dusted them herself every morning after breakfast, with great rapidity, while Lucy was allowed to crawl round the legs of the chairs, and Delia, with a feather duster, flicked at the Dresden china on the mantelpiece.

"Delia's a good careful girl, and her eyes are better than mine," said Shân briskly. But though Delia was certainly good and tried to be careful, the petals of the roses and carnations had a way of snapping off now and then, and the china apple tree, in whose shade sat a plump, fair lady and an elegant gentleman in a plum-coloured suit, holding a watch in his hand, was pruned in time of nearly all its apples. Shân was annoyed when this happened, but her anger, though fierce, never lasted long.

In the Poet's drawing-room there was neither "silver table" nor china ornament. Almost the only pictures in the room were over the fireplace, where naked men rode and led prancing horses. The Poet called them the "Parthenon frieze," and said they came from Greece, and that the people who made them were the only ones who understood the meaning of beauty. Secretly Lucy thought that Shân's Dresden china gentlemen in their crimson breeches, buckled shoes and three-cornered hats were far more beautiful. And yet there was no doubt that the Poet's room was a very good sort of place. On the wall above the piano hung two white faces—the death-masks, said the Poet, of Dante and Beethoven. They had a secret look, like the hills which Lucy watched from her window in the early morning, when they had seen the sunrise before the rest of the world.

But nothing in the room impressed Lucy more than the number of its books. They were everywhere— climbing to the ceiling on high shelves, lying in heaps on the tables, dribbling on to chairs and piled in corners of the floor. How could anyone, Delia and Lucy asked each other, find time to read so many books, particularly such a man as the Poet, who was clearly in need of none, since his head was completely full of fairy stories? It was all very well for ordinary grown-ups, who appeared to have no heads at all when you asked them for a tale, to resort to books; but no book ever contained so many entertaining, puzzling, enthralling adventures as the Poet related for Delia's and Lucy's delight.

Shân was fond of giving tea-parties. The children found
her grown-up variety—of which there were a great many—
very tiresome. Wearing starched pinafores, their curls
carefully brushed round Louisa's fingers (a long and
sickening process), they descended to the hall and stood for a
few moments outside the drawing-room door, listening to the
extraordinary babel of sound coming from the other side. In
one minute they would be standing in the middle of the room,
surrounded on every side by ladies with quizzical eyes under
their high hats, ladies with bags and bracelets, drawing
slippery kid gloves over their ringed fingers, and the children
must go from one to the other, while voices exclaimed: "How
they've grown!" (Would there ever come a day when people
would no longer say that?) All these trials were waiting for
them behind the closed door, while out here, in the lamplit
hall, it was quiet and kind, with only the friendly sound of
Kate washing up the tea-things in the pantry.

"Go you in now, all of you!" said Louisa's hoarse whisper
over the banisters. "See that Maurice remembers his right
hand. And mind you behave!"

With that Delia opened the door and for a moment the
noise of voices died down and all the heads and hats were
turned in their direction.

Decidedly that was the worst kind of party, even bearing
marks of shame as when Maurice would hang his head and
refuse to say How do you do; while Miriam one day, suddenly
beholding the Poet, marooned among the ladies, had made
herself horribly conspicuous by crying out "Man! Man!" and
rushing across the room into his arms. Lucy's blackest
moment came at a time when she was told to pass the bread
and butter to Mrs. Hughes-Jenkins. Wrapped in a dream of the
Innocent Child and her latest torment she took the plate and
approached the stout figure on the sofa. The Innocent Child
had been betrayed once more ("Agony! Ebony! Mahogany!"
went the refrain in Lucy's head: a pleasing new invention

which she must remember to repeat to Delia). Her pride was still unbroken, her noble head unbent, yet her captors were pressing round her, and with that the entire plateful of bread-and-butter slipped, slid and landed, butter side down, on Mrs. Hughes-Jenkins's satin lap. Oh, dark and miserable day! Even the Innocent Child might have quailed on hearing all that Shân had to say. Agony! Ebony! Mahogany!

There was also the kind of party where grown-ups and children mingled and when, after a nursery tea with one of Shan's sponge cakes—light as sea-foam, yellow as a gorse-bush—youthful guests and hosts descended together to the drawing-room to entertain their elders with charades and recitations. Delia would repeat "Abou ben Adhem, may his tribe increase!", while Lucy had to content herself with "Lord Ullin's Daughter" and "The Skeleton in Armour," her favourite "Barbara Fritchie" having been unfairly filched by Maurice, who won great applause by shouting out the lines:

> "Who touches a hair of yon grey head,
> Dies like a dog!"

But none of them could compete with Perceval Tudor, who came with his French governess- a dark and slatternly woman with her blouse gaping at the back. No sooner had he finished "The Wreck of the Hesperus" and

> "Men may come and men may go,
> But I go on for ever,"

than Mademoiselle would cry out: "Alors, Perceval, dis donc tes fables de La Fontaine!", and off he would go again, though no one could understand a word, and Shân had fallen asleep long ago. When she woke up she would say:

"Thank you, Perceval, that will do nicely. Now out you all go and do a charade"—and then it really was fun. There was very little stage property in the hall, none of those coats and hats and riding-crops which were so valuable at Pengarth; but much might be done with antimacassars from the dining-room, and sometimes a hat or veil of Shân's from upstairs.

The third kind of party—and the best—took place entirely in the nursery, without parents, aunts or governesses. If the guests were girls they brought out their dolls, and Maurice was the father, or, more often, the doctor, arriving with a bag and a piece of rubber tubing which looked a little like a stethoscope. Or, if the visitors were boys and of the right calibre, they would play shipwreck, with brooms for masts, and for rigging a piece of braid that had once gone round the bottom of their mother's skirt and now stretched the whole length of the room. Then they would suffer storm and shipwreck, casting themselves violently from the back of the leather armchair on to the floor with cries of "Codho!", while the survivors were restored with those pink and yellow sweets called "Hundreds and Thousands," placed on the outstretched tongue. Miriam was not allowed to be a sailor because she easily got hurt, but they let her keep the shop which stocked the "Hundreds and Thousands," and as this was rather dull, they gave her some paper and coloured chalks to keep her quiet.

If there was a drawback to Shân's house it was the scarcity of books. Apart from those which were dusted so carefully every morning on the drawing-room table, from which small good could be got, there was little to fall back on on wet days when the books they had brought with them from home were exhausted. (Louisa was stingy when it came to packing books.)

The nursery shelf was of small use. It held a copy of "Little Arthur's England" and a stumpy dark green book called "The Gates Ajar," where the characters talked but never really did anything, and a faded, yellow-leaved "Medical Handbook" where, on the contrary, they did the most surprising things. But there were days when Lucy in particular longed for the books at home: for "Undine" and "The Last of the Mohicans," and the green-and-gold regiment of the Waverley Novels in the library, and the Crimson Fairy Book with all its coloured companions in the sitting-room upstairs, where she could sit and read, hidden yet with one ear cocked for Louisa's voice. Why didn't Shân keep some poetry; something that one cauld learn by heart besides the Bible on Sundays? In desperation Lucy was reduced to memorising any scrap of print she could find on any of the pictures, from the plump Titian Venus in the bathroom, to the "English Farm Yard" in her bedroom. She would repeat them to Delia, who was a great stickler for accuracy.

"Now listen, Delia, is this right? 'An English Farm Yard. Painted by J. F. Herring. Engraved by G. Patterson. Copyright entered according to the Act of Congress by William Stevens Williams Co. in the Clerk's office of the District Court for the Southern District of New York.' "

But in one respect Shân's library made generous amends for its limitations. On one side of the drawing-room fireplace, under the grey-and-gold Worcester china on its triple shelves, stood two rows of the bound volumes of Punth. No day could be altogether dull when these could be carried to the sofa or hearth-rug, and through the long lamp-lit evenings, or on wet Sunday afternoons when Shân dozed in her armchair, and the people passed by under their umbrellas to Sunday School, and the rainy wind moaned down the chimney, Delia and Lucy lived contentedly in a world peopled by crinolined ladies, "Hunting gents," and "Returning revellers" in stove-pipe hats who made remarks full of "Sh's" that were hard to follow; and, best of all, by Sir Gorgius Midas, Mrs. Ponsonby de Tomkins, Duchesses with lofty noses and beautiful, tall young women. The printed pages were disappointingly dull and difficult, but the cartoons were excellent company. Delia and

Lucy could recognise at a glance Mr. Gladstone, sometimes dressed as a schoolmistress, scolding Lord Randolph Churchill; Dizzy, with his curls, playing with an Egyptian Puzzle, and Lord Palmerston holding a straw in his mouth—though no one could tell them why.

Chapter Nine

The House by the Sea

Part II

From the west window in the nursery—that corner window which had the best view of all—the children could watch the quay and beyond it the line of breaking foam which hid the bar. Once a fortnight the steamship "Laura" would heave in sight, and that meant, as often as not, that the sack of flour which Shân had ordered from Liverpool and the bag of potatoes from Ireland would soon be unloaded and delivered at the door—for that was the way in which Shân did part of her shopping.

The "Laura" came so often that her skipper knew where to cross the bar without going aground on a sandbank. But whenever a lovely Norwegian schooner appeared like a bird on the horizon she had to wait for the pilot, Captain Owen, with his oilskins and his gold earrings, to go out in his boat, board her and bring her safely in. And then, if the day were fine and Louisa willing, the children might hasten down to the quay with the rest of the village, to watch the schooner come alongside, Captain Owen standing proudly on the bridge beside the Norwegian captain, and the yellow-haired crew running about uncoiling ropes and calling to each other in their foreign tongue. During the next day or two the sailors would be busy unloading the white, sweet-smelling timber; and on Sunday, with their pink faces scrubbed and wearing their trim blue jerseys, they stood about uncertainly in the street.

Now and then, as a treat, Shân would have the altogether excellent idea of hiring a boat, and then Delia or Lucy would be despatched hot-foot to the fishermen who sat on a bench or leant on the wall at the end of the quay. At the timid mention of a boat they would gaze ruefully at the sky.

"A sailing-boat, please," Lucy would add, if she were the messenger—knowing full well that Shân had meant a rowing-boat. At the word "sailing" profound gloom would spread over the faces before her.

"Is Auntie coming?"

"Of course she is."

"Well now, there's a nice little rowing-boat, what-ever. John Willie will be bringing her opposite Auntie's house at half-past two. The wind and tide's no good at all for sailing to-day."

But sometimes Lucy got her way, and Shân, in anger, would observe the top of a sail from her window.

"If that silly bobbin John Willie hasn't brought his old sailing-boat! She's not fit for anyone, I tell you. I'm not coming!"

But, of course, they knew she would come. And John Willie knew she would come. And Shân knew that John Willie knew that she would come. But how sharp a zest was added to the venture when Shân, her hat swathed in a white motoring-veil, picked her way over the pebbles in her tiny kid shoes (no one had such small feet as Shân), protesting at the madness of the whole idea, screaming aloud when John Willie hoisted her over the bows with "Never you fear, Ma'am!", followed by the gleeful children wrapped in an assortment of scarves, capes, gaiters and spencers of shapeless wool, for there was an idea—firmly planted in the heads of the grown-ups—that it was always "chilly" on the water. Had John Willie's boat overturned, her cargo of padded passengers would have bobbed on the surface like so many buoys; but they always came safely home again, turning back just as the foaming bar and open sea were reached. Lucy, sitting ecstatically in the bows, listening to the sound of the water as it rushed gurgling beneath her, was sure that the boat minded as much as she did, that some wild, free spirit died, as it died within her breast, when John Willie put his helm over and the west wind that had come to meet them fell suddenly away.

But Shân was happy once more. From her seat in the stern she could look at the green hills, the houses climbing up them, admire her own sun-blinds and window-boxes and white front door, observe that Mrs. Hughes-Jenkins's chimney was on fire and that Colonel Frazer had painted his summer-house pink. John Willie held the tiller and chewed tobacco while he related the gossip of the village. Sometimes the children would get him to tell his adventures, for he was an old seafaring man and had been as far as Marseilles, where he had learnt a little French. It was confined to three remarks: "Partez demain"; "Partez ce soir"; "Café et cognac."

*   *   *

On Sunday mornings there were two possibilities for Delia and Lucy. Either they would accompany Shân to church, or their mother—if she had not gone with their father to such far-away regions as France or Italy— would take them to the Welsh chapel.

Church was like one more of Shân's tea-parties, with all the same people dressed up in the same clothes. Except for the Ten Commandments, which were written up on the walls in Welsh, everything was in English. The church had none of the friendly dimness of Pengarth: it was bare and ugly and full of strong reflected light from the water outside; instead of pews there were rows of yellow chairs that shifted and shot forward when you leant on them to pray. Delia and Lucy and even Maurice were used to sitting through a sermon without too much fidgeting, but Shân was delighted to have an excuse for escape. At the final verse of the preceding hymn she would begin nodding and raising her eyebrows at the children; at the middle verse she dropped briskly on her knees and bent her head for a minute in prayer; by the last verse she was up again, had gathered her bag and umbrella together, in piercing whispers directed Lucy not to leave her mackintosh and Prayer Book behind, and, as the choir sang Amen, headed a shamefaced procession of children down the aisle. If only they had not sat so near the front they could have borne it better.

"It's a good idea, Shân," said Colonel Frazer. "You might lend me one of those children next Sunday."

But Shân only laughed.

Chapel was different. No question there of evading the sermon, since it was what everyone had come to hear. Delia and Lucy, who did not understand more than a word here and there, were allowed to read the book of Esther to themselves, but even the Arabian Night adventures of Ahasuerus and Mordecai paled before the diversion of listening to Mr. Evan Thomas. No sermon that Delia and Lucy understood was half so good as Mr. Thomas's sounded. When his voice rose to a hwyl, they sat rigid with excitement: his eyes burning like black coals, his pale face shining with the light of vision, the deformity of his shrivelled right hand forgotten in the sweeping gestures of his left arm, Mr. Thomas was like the Prophet Elijah. Then swiftly, from that high soaring flight where the spirit beat its wings against the door of Heaven, his voice would drop, straight as a plumb-line, into ordinary speech, and the sudden change sent a shiver down their spines, while old Danny Morris, who sat under the pulpit, called out a fervent "Amen!"

But if the sermons were good the hymns were even better, for Delia and Lucy could at least read their Welsh hymn-books. The tunes were glorious and familiar—full of wind and sea and hilly places—and the voices, singing in parts, fitted the tunes and loved them so that it seemed they could not bear to leave them, lingering tenderly on the last verse, repeating it with rapture—again and again.

There was only one church in the village, but so many chapels that the children had never succeeded in counting them all and never could remember which was which. One of them—an English chapel—stood close beside Shân's garden, and they would sit reading their story-books in the summer-house on Sunday evenings to the sound of "Lead, Kindly Light" and "For ever with the Lord." Blue water and bluer hills were framed in climbing roses, and the apples, ripening placidly in the sun, made a green pattern of fruit and leaves through which appeared the line of white foam, breaking lazily on the bar, and far beyond it the remote spaces of the sea.

*   *   *

It was while she was staying in Shân's house that Lucy began the strange habit of "remembering"—a thing she could not even explain to Delia. At the end of the hot morning, walking back from the sands, she would drag her spade along the iron chain that edged the sea-wall, so that it made a jiggy feeling all the way up her arm, and think: "I shall remember this, and how thirsty I am, and the way my arm jigs and shakes." Later, in the cool dining-room, drinking tepid water out of her Coronation mug, that same thought—"I shall remember this"—would recur, just as it did when she lay after lunch on the drawing-room floor with Punch, Shân snoring lightly in the chair, the sun-blinds down and only a little of the bright water reflected upwards in the dim room, with its china and pictures and the box of ivory dominoes—the Double Five missing. All over the ceiling were wreaths of wild roses, tied with fluttering green ribbons, and if she opened the bottom of the Welsh tridarn—but, of course, she never would—softly, softly, so as not to waken Shân, there might be peppermints there on a little silver dish, and in the bottom of the cupboard a slight smell of camphor.

These things, like the butterflies hovering in the sunny garden, refused to be caught and pinned down; but they were gay and cheerful and part of the cosiness that belonged to Shân. Yet there were some pieces in the pattern that were not gay at all. Shân playing the piano, with a touch as light as a breeze, could find airs and scraps of tunes that made you cry. There were days when Lucy, chalking picture-books on the floor by the nursery window, was suddenly frightened by the sound of feet on the pavement; so frightened that it took all her courage to stay where she was and not go running from the room. Even Louisa, after a long visit, was invaded by melancholy.

The children stayed there one long autumn and winter while their parents were abroad. Miriam was ailing and would not sleep at night unless Louisa rocked and sang her to sleep in her arms. One of the songs was about a poor flower-girl whom everyone passed by in the street while she stood there friendless—

> Crying all this night so bitter:
> "Won't you buy my pretty flowers?"

And Lucy, eating her bread-and-milk under the lamp at the nursery table, aghast at the thought of that forsaken flower-girl, knew that she would always remember this: Miriam's yellow head against Louisa's shoulder, and outside in the darkness the wind and the waves, the street lamp shining uncertainly on the dark water, and the rain that drove all night against the window.

CHILDREN ON THE CROQUET LAWN

With motley balls through battered hoops
They wage their long campaign;
Beneath the oak tree's dreaming shade
The drowsy doves complain;
The daisied lawn, where now they roam,
An ocean seems, white-flecked with foam.

O Time, stand stilll O Fate, forbear
To strike so hard and true!
A little longer let them sport
Who reek not yet of you,
Who think the world is made for play
And Life an endless summer day.

Chapter Ten

A Day of Her Own

It was a March morning. Delia and Maurice had driven from Pengarth to the station with Beedles and Miss Crabtree after breakfast to catch the train for Dewbury, where, in Miss Crabtree's charge, they were to spend the day visiting the dentist. They had set out cheerfully, Maurice having been promised a new engine if he behaved well and opened his mouth wide; while Delia, who was too old and wise for bribery, was buoyed up by the thought of lunch at Trimmer's Tea Shop, where the pillars were made of green glass and the waitresses wore pink frocks and bows on their heads. She had already decided to choose a meringue for her second course.

Lucy had run all the way down the drive for the fun of opening the big iron gates for Beedles, and had stood in the road waving until the dog-cart with its freight of passengers perched aloft—Maurice safely tucked between Beedles and Miss Crabtree, and Delia clinging to the back seat—had swung briskly round the bend, whereupon a sense of flatness and staleness invaded her. Why did her teeth show no inclination to stick out like Maurice's, or develop holes, revealed by the eating of toffee, as Delia's did? For them was reserved the thrill of a railway journey into England; the sight of shops and houses and people jostling each other on the pavement; the hushed grandeur of the dentist's waiting-room, where Delia reported that there were copies of Punch, much duller than Shân's and containing no mention of either Disraeli or Mrs. Ponsonby de Tomkins.

Pondering these things and the unfairness of fate, Lucy returned slowly up the drive under the clamour of the building rooks who, with their usual untidiness, had strewn the ground

with far more sticks than were necessary for the building of
their nests. The day lay before her—a coloured plaything with
which to do as she chose. Already it seemed a little brighter
than it had been at the moment when first she found herself
alone; already in her mind's eye she perceived a vista of
green, wet fields shining with rain and sun, of dark and
cobwebbed outbuildings, scented with the smell of horses'
and cows' breath, the feel of Indian corn slipping slowly
through her fingers, the delicious stirring of pigs' food, the
possibility—remote and rapturous—of a rat hunt.

There is no better place for contemplation than a swinging
gate, and Lucy turned her steps to the iron gate at the top of
the stable-yard, from where, floating pleasantly through the
air while with one expert foot she accelerated and slackened
her pace, she could listen to the chatter of the maids in the
wash-house. Now and then one of them would come out to
draw fresh rain-water from the great butt that stood beside the
door, while a plume of blue smoke from the boiler fire curled
upwards through the chimney against the naked branches of
the trees.

"Now then, Miss Lucy," said Jarman's croaking voice,
"you'll have the hinges off that gate if you're not careful.
How many times has Beedles told you not to go a-swinging,"

Lucy disliked Jarman when he talked in that way. He was
standing in front of her with a bunch of leeks in his hands
which he was taking to the kitchen, but he did not even wait
to see whether or not she stopped swinging (which was
annoying, since she would like to have defied him), but
hurried away to the house. She went on swinging for a few
minutes, hoping he would return, but he remained indoors
talking to Mrs. Bannister, and at last Lucy, deciding that she
was no longer amused, stepped off the gate and went slowly
down the yard, pausing, on her way, to jump from the top of
the stone mounting-block.

At the stable door she hesitated a moment. The near stall

was empty since Fancy had gone to the station with the dog-cart; in the farther one Beauty fidgeted and pulled at her head-stall, hearing Lucy's footsteps. The saddle-room door was beyond and, knowing Beedles to be safely out of it, Lucy would have liked to go in, for it was a pleasant place with its raftered ceiling and smell of saddle-soap, its polished harness hanging behind holland curtains, and its perpetually surprising view of the river through the ivied window, where Beedles brushed his hair before a dim and spotted mirror. But Beauty's shifting hind-quarters were uncomfortably near the saddle-room door and Lucy was an arrant coward in the matter of a horse's hind legs. She longed for the courage to shout, "Get over, horse!" the way Beedles did, but not possessing it, she turned away.

From the open outer door of the loose box came a soft whinny. Black Prince stirred in the shadows as Lucy looked in, and thrust his velvet nose into her hand. She rubbed it and gave him a twist of hay. Then she went on into the cow-yard. The green and golden moss on the cart-shed roof shone in the clear spring sunlight. It was, Lucy thought, nearly as good to look at as the ginger-bread roof must have been in the story of Hansel and Gretel. She went into the cow-house, picking her way carefully over the golden-brown runnels, for the cows were messy in their habits.

In the corner of the dark shed something moved and got up hurriedly, with great commotion, from the bottom of its pen, and a little red-and-white calf stood looking at Lucy, its knees trembling, its head moving slowly from side to side like an old bull. As she moved nearer it bounded away to the far side, hitting its head crack against the wall. Lucy stood quite still, one hand pushed through the bars, and after two or three minutes the calf came slowly towards her, watching her under its white lashes. Lucy stretched her fingers very carefully and the calf stopped short and blew out its breath; then delicately and cautiously it pushed its head forward and extended the tip of its tongue. Lucy did not move. The calf drew back for a moment, then changed its mind and returned; nor did it waste any more time, but stood butting Lucy with its wet nose, curling its tongue round her ftngers, tasting with relish the faint saltiness of the palm of her hand. She could see the coarse white curls on its forehead and the tiny tips of its growing horns. And still, as she leaned over the pen, enjoying the scent of hay and calf's breath and the feel of that warm, rough tongue, her day and all its possibilities stood before her —young and hesitating as the ungainly calf.

She thought: 'First I shall skip all round the garden,' and, with that, she ran out into the sunshine and back to the house as fast as her legs could carry her. She found her skipping-rope in the corner of the nursery cupboard and was out again before Louisa could cry a warning about getting her feet wet. This time she avoided the stable yard and went instead through the shrubbery, and so out of the little wicket into the paddock. The green spears of the daffodils stood up straight through the grass and some of the bees had ventured out from their hives into the sunshine. Lucy opened the white door in the wall and stepped into the kitchen garden. Then she began to skip.

First she skipped slowly towards the corner by the potting-shed; the path was damp and muddy here, since it was sheltered from the sun, and her skipping-rope went "slap, slap" on the wet ground. At the potting-shed she stopped to talk to Tom Tiddler, the garden cat—a grey, aloof creature— and she ran her fingers through the Indian corn which Jarman kept for the ducks. She had been looking forward to this for some time. There was nothing of interest on Jarman's table to-day, only a seed catalogue, his pruning-knife and a china cup. It was still too early to watch him fry his bacon for dinner, so Lucy went out again and skipped up the garden path. The beds on either side of the path were bare and dark and wet; there were no leaves showing on the gooseberry bushes, and the asparagus bed—which had provided cover for hide and seek all autumn—had been cut down long ago. It was dull in the garden to-day. Perhaps, Lucy thought, there would be a frog in the pond, and sure enough there was one, squatting on the bottom step of the ladder. Lucy tickled him with a long grass, but he did not mind, so she banged the ladder on the bottom of the pond, at which the frog fell in with a splash and swam away, his legs moving like a pair of scissors.

Then Lucy skipped down Trotty Hill. (They called it this, but no one knew why.) She said to herself, "I am skipping fast and well," and she threw back her head and lifted her feet neatly, swinging the rope clear so that it did not catch the box edge on either side of the path. But when she reached the rhubarb pots standing in their yellow straw, she grew suddenly bored with the garden. If Maurice had been there to play trains or horses it would have been a different matter, but this was a day of her own; it was stupid to stay between four walls. So she turned and skipped back to the top of the garden. There was another door here in the warm south wall, where peaches and greengages ripened in the summer-time. Lucy leant for a moment against the door, feeling its heat on her back; the white paint hung in dry flakes which she could pull off with her fingers, and the boards were pitted with lead shot—marks of Jarman's attempts to shoot a jay which was eating his peas. A delicate, dreamy scent rose in the air from somewhere near her feet; Lucy bent down and, parting the leaves, discovered some white violets. She thought she would pick them for her mother and put them on her dressing-table as a surprise; but not now. There was too much to do, and with that she opened the door, which stuck a little in the long grass, and stepped out on to the hillside.

The first thing Lucy did when she was the other side of the wall was to knot her skipping-rope round her waist so that it resembled a cartridge-belt, and then draw the elastic of her hat on to her chin. The Volunteers, when they marched past to camp in the summer, wore their chin-straps in this position, and the feel of the elastic on her lower jaw gave her immediately a fierce and slightly military sensation. In view of the long campaign before her she tightened her belt by making another knot in her skipping-rope. Then she chose a pea-stick from the pile which Jarman had left against the wall, and with this—her "longue carabine" as she called it—over her shoulder, she set out warily across the Banky Field, keeping a sharp look-out on either side.

"The Last of the Mohicans" was a favourite book, and chief of its characters was "Hawk-Eye," "Leather Jacket," or "La Longue Carabine." His names were as baffling as his personality; often he was referred to simply as "that extraordinary man," and as that Lucy liked to think of herself while she made her way across the fields, studying the ground for footprints (but there never were any footprints in the grass) and steering her course by the sun (which remained obstinately in the same place overhead). It was a pity that Delia or Maurice was not there to take the part of Chingach gook; as it was she must push on alone through the forest on her task of rescuing the ladies Cora and Alice from the Huron tribe. When she came to the white gate into the hayfield, she did not climb it, but glided noiselessly, Indian fashion, through the gap in the hedge. A rabbit, who had been sunning himself on the far side, popped into his hole in a Hurry and Lucy exclaimed "Huh!", which was Chingachgook's favourite expression. She then continued creeping along the hedge, her carabine cocked, while with her hawk-eye she raked the bare twigs for the first sign of a hedge-sparrow's nest;but of course Delia would find one first—she always did.

The river ran round two sides of the hayfield, making at one corner a tiny strand of gravel and grey sand under the willows. Here, to her joy, Hawk-Eye discovered little tracks leading to the water's edge. Silently, and on tiptoe, she followed them, stooping under the catkined hazels, crawling beneath twisted tree-roots. The tracks ended under an alder tree, and out of it, with a scuffle and a flounce, tumbled a moor-hen into the water -below.

"Huh!" said Lucy, and the moor-hen fussed, helterskelter, across the river, a silver trail spreading in its wake. "La Longue Carabine" raised her rifle to her shoulder, then lowered it and stood leaning on her weapon while the river swirled past her feet, brown with the winter floods save where the water caught, like a gleaming shield, the spring sky above. Then she turned and silently made her way upstream.

The floods had gone down, leaving a rim along the bank and a dark fringe of sticks and straw by which it was not difficult to trace the Hurons. The lower branches of the willows were wreathed in straws and dead leaves, hanging twisted and dried like the scalps of an enemy. Beside their dusty dreariness the pussywillow and the lambs' tails on the nut bushes were silver and gold, and Lucy, forgetting "that extraordinary man," began to make a song about them.

> The river runs fast to meet the sea,
> Sticks and straws for the willow tree,
> But silver and gold for you and me.

Not a very good song, she thought, but the tune was all right. Just at that moment out flew a kingfisher from the willow tree and darted across the river, a blue arrow in the sunshine, shooting into furthermost space. Lucy finished her song as she climbed the bank:

> Silver for me and gold for you,
> The river is brown and the kingfisher blue;
> Out of the willow it flew, it flew!

Miriam was playing with Maurice's cart and horse. Coming up from the river bank Lucy found her engaged in putting gravel into the cart with her wooden spade, while Robert, the cart-horse, watched the proceeding with a glassy eye.

"Would you like me to play with you?" asked Lucy.

"Do' want to play," said Miriam. "I'se busy."

"But you're only filling that old cart with gravel. And, anyway, it will all fall out as soon as you pull Robert along."

Miriam went on filling the cart. In her three-anda-half years of existence she had learnt to mistrust Lucy's suggestions. This suspicion annoyed Lucy; in her most cooing voice she began again:

"If you come with me I'll show you a much better game than that ever so much better."

Miriam went on digging gravel.

"We'll go into the prairies, and wander in the forests, till we come to streams that flow towards the summer. And I'll make you a feast from the flesh of deer and fish from the Great Lakes," she improvised rapidly. "Honey of wild bees and cold mushrooms and all the most exquisite things you ever tasted."

"Where," asked Miriam, putting down her spade.

"Oh, just over there in the field," said Lucy airily. "But you must leave Robert and come with me."

Miriam sighed. Then she bent down, patted Robert's dusty mane and kissed his painted forehead. "I'll be back soon, darling," Lucy heard her say.

They set off together across the lawn, and when they came to the railings Lucy climbed over them and pulled Miriam through the bars into the field the other side. Lucy, by this time, was a little tired of "that extraordinary man" and his acute observations; a game with Miriam, she thought, would be a pleasant change. They went on until they reached the giant oak tree near the road, and there Lucy made the promised feast with chopped leaves and primroses picked from under the hedge, while Miriam laid the table with bits of stick and stone and last year's acorn cups.

Then Lucy had another idea.

"Miriam, let's pretend that you're my little girl, and now that we've had supper I shall undress you and put you to bed."

"'Do' want to go to bed," said Miriam.

"Oh yes, Mirie. Look, it's ever such a soft bed under the tree, lined with moss and leaves like a fairy's cradle, and I'll undress you properly!"

She took off Miriam's coat and shoes, her blue smock and her white frilly petticoat.

"You can keep on your flannel petticoat," said Lucy, "it looks rather like a nightgown. Now curl up and go to sleep and I'll come back in a minute with a surprise."

Miriam lay down obediently on the ground, screwing up her eyes, and Lucy ran away. She intended returning in a few minutes disguised as a fairy and ready to offer Miriam one of three wishes, but the field lay beckoning to her with so fair a look that she was loth to turn back.

Swept clean by the March winds the grass, not yet grown after the long winter, stretched invitingly from the glittering hollies on the bank, across the ridge of the Roman Road that ran, straight as an arrow, between the two fords of the river, to the far corner by the twisted thorn trees where Lucy could see Jenny, the terrier, quietly rabbiting on her own. Beyond the hedge Jim Gethin was ploughing, with a flurry of white seagulls following him and his two horses, and in the corner of their own field Davey John was busy hedging. By his side was a bundle of sharp sticks, and whenever he planted one in the ground with his gloved hand he would knock it firmly on the head with his bill-hook.

"Good morning, Davey John," called out Lucy.

"Morning, Miss Lucy. Nice fine day it is. But there'll be rain, I doubt, soon as ever the sun and the wind get together." And he took up another stake.

"Davey John, aren't you tired of doing that?" asked Lucy.

"Well now, I dunno," said Davey John, standing still and scratching his head. "I dare say you get tired of your book-learning now and then."

"Dreadfully," said Lucy. "Especially French verbs. Did you, when you were at school?"

"Well now, I dunno as I heard tell of them," Davey pondered. "But they do say," he went on, "that when I was a boy I was right sharp at figures."

"If you mean sums, I think they're devilish," said Lucy. "When I'm grown up I shall write an arithmetic book full of the most awful questions with no answers, and I shall give it to all the people I hate most."

Davey John went on driving stakes into the ground, and Lucy sat down on a bundle of sticks, prepared to carry on the conversation.

"Delia is better at arithmetic than I am," she continued. "And David Vaughan is like you; I mean right sharp at figures. That's what you said, didn't you? I don't mind English grammar so much because the pieces of parsing are taken out of real books, but history is the only lesson I really like because it's about people. D'you know, Davey John, that Henry VII probably came through this field on his way to the Battle of Bosworth? Wouldn't you like to have been there, marching into England with a Welsh army.,—though I can't say that Henry VII is one of my favourite kings."

Davey John drew the thorns carefully together.

"There's clever you are to know all that," he remarked.

"Oh, that's nothing to what I could tell you," said Lucy modestly. "The Civil War is the best time; I wish I had lived then. David Vaughan would have joined the Cavaliers, but I'd have been a Roundhead, wouldn't you, Davey John?"

"I'd have come with you, Miss Lucy. I can't say no more than that, can I?"

"That's nice of you," she said gravely. "Delia's a

Roundhead too, and so would Maurice and Miriam be if we told them to come along."

Then she suddenly remembered Miriam.

"Would you mind coming with me now, at once?" she said, getting up hastily. "I've promised Miriam a surprise, and you can be the surprise if you like."

"Well now, I dunno as how I should be much of a surprise," said Davey John.

"Oh yes, you'll do. Please come quick."

Davey John put down his bill-hook and walked slowly and squashily beside Lucy. But when they reached the oak tree Miriam was no longer curled up on the ground. She was standing in the middle of the field and the tears were running down her plump cheeks on to the front of her flannel petticoat.

"Oh, Miriam, you should have stayed in bed," Lucy called out. "I've got a surprise for you."

"'do want a surprise. I want Louisa!" wailed Miriam.

"Jowks!" exclaimed Davey John. "Whatever kind of game are you playing at, Miss Lucy?"

"Oh, just an ordinary game. Miriam was my little girl and I undressed her and put her to bed."

"'do want to go to bed," howled Miriam. "I want Louisa."

``Why, whatever would your ma say, and Louisa too?" said Davey John. "There's real wicked you are, Miss Lucy, to go taking off your poor little sister's clothes in this wind, and settin' her down in them damp old leaves to catch her death of cold. She's fair starved, I shouldn't wonder."

Lucy had never heard Davey John talk like that before. By this time the sun was hidden in clouds and the bright colours of the day had faded. She gathered Miriam's clothes together and she and Davey John began dressing her as well as they could, but the string of the frilly white petticoat had got into a knot which Davey John's big fingers could not unfasten. All the time Miriam was crying loudly and the people passing along the road in their traps on the way to market turned their heads and looked over the hedge.

They were still trying to undo the knot when the groaning of the big iron gates fell on their ears. An open barouche drawn by a grey horse was turning into the drive, and seated behind were two ladies whom Lucy, with one horrified glance, recognised as Mrs. Williams Thomas and her sister, Miss Pumphrey.

"Oh; Davey John, look quick! Whatever shall we do? It's Mrs. Williams Thomas!"

"I don't care if it's the Queen of England herself," said Davey John grimly. "I'm fair moidered with these strings and buttons, drat them! Hush your hollerin' now, bach," he added to Miriam.

But there was no silencing Miriam; she cried seldom, but whole-heartedly, and the stately progress of the barouche up the drive was arrested. One of the ladies was stepping out of the carriage as Davey John, grown desperate, broke the string and pulled the petticoat over Miriam's head. Her crimson, puckered face reappeared the other side at the same time as Miss Pumphrey was seen to be advancing over the grass.

"What has happened?" she called out. "Is somebody hurt? Why, it's Lucy and Miriam!" she added, peering short-sightedly in front of her. "Has Miriam fallen down?"

"She's all right, Mum," said Davey John, fastening on the blue smock back to front. "She's not hurt, only cold and a bit feared-like."

"What an extraordinary thing!" said Miss Pumphrey. "We had better drive her up to the house. Is your mother at home, Lucy?"

Lucy did not answer. She was too much ashamed. Davey John picked up Miriam and carried her to the carriage, and Lucy—abandoning the search for one of Miriam's shoes—walked behind. Miss Pumphrey hurried on ahead.

"What is the matter, Clara?" asked Mrs. Williams Thomas

impatiently, as the procession approached. She was a handsome lady and always dressed in purple. Lucy was frightened of her dark eyes and deep voice.

"I don't quite know, dear," said Miss Pumphrey. "But I think we had better take Miriam home in the carriage." She looked disapprovingly at Davey John.

"Certainly. She can sit between us," said Mrs. Williams Thomas.

But they had reckoned without Miriam. With a shriek she Hung her arms round Davey John's neck, and nothing—no cajolement or remonstrance from the ladies—would move her.

"I'd best take her myself," said Davey John.

"Very well. Drive on, James," said Mrs. Williams Thomas tartly, and the barouche bowled away up the drive, followed slowly by the three.

Davey John said nothing. Lucy hung her head, and Miriam's whole body was shaken with sobs. They could see the ladies alighting at the front door as they made their way towards the shrubbery and the back door of the house, where Louisa was waiting to receive them.

In the night nursery, where she spent the whole of the afternoon, Lucy considered her wretchedness and the ruin of her day. Looking back on it, she remembered the pleasant movement of the swinging gate; the lovely moment when the calf overcame its fear and licked her hand; the cool dribbling of the Indian corn between her fingers; the scent of the white violets by the garden door; the manly feeling of the rope round her waist and the elastic under her chin; the sight of the moor-hen's tiny footmarks on the sandy shore and the flash of the kingfisher across the river. All that time she had been particularly happy, even when she was talking to Davey John about Cavaliers and Roundheads while poor Miriam was shivering under the tree; and she might have been happy now if only she had not spoilt it all! Dick had promised to make a catapult for her, and that very afternoon Jarman would be burning the old laurel bush which he had cut down of late, and she would not be there to watch the long flames leap in the air, or hear the crackle and hiss as the leaves twisted and blackened and the moisture ran from them in little drops.

Then she might have picked the white violets for her mother, arranging them in the blue jug she liked and carrying them very quietly up the front stairs to her room as a surprise. And now instead she was shut up in the night nursery, which she hated, with nothing to do, nothing to look at except the picture of William Shakespeare over the wash-stand, with a tassel like the end of a blind-cord round his neck, and Louisa's ugly brown pincushion on the chest of drawers.

"I won't cry," she said to herself. "I won't." And she leaned her face against the cold window-pane and looked out into the garden. The rooks were beginning to sweep home to their nests. She saw Dick come out of the paddock and jump the railings into the field with Jenny at his heels. In the corner of the shrubbery a thin column of blue smoke rose into the air: Jarman had lit his bonfire. Then trees, garden and-field swam together as the tears rushed into Lucy's eyes and splashed on the window-sill.

Davey John found Miriam's shoe next day; one of the cows had trodden on it and licked the rosette off the toe.

Chapter Eleven

The Harpist

Jack Baba, the black-and-white rabbit, was growing old and slow in his ways. He was too fat and heavy to carry far, and Maurice invented a method of pushing a stick under his hind legs: tipped on his nose, Jack Baba was obliged to hop forwards, and by these means his progress along the garden paths was hastened. But although he was tedious and sometimes cantankerous they all loved him, and never contemplated a day when he would be no longer there.

One morning Delia, who had gone out early to feed and water the rabbits and guinea-pigs, burst into the nursery with a white face and round, staring eyes.

"He's dead!" she cried. "And I didn't know it. I picked him up, but he was cold and all floppy, and he's dead!"

"For pity's sake, what is it? Who's dead?" asked Louisa sharply.

"Jack Baba," said Delia, still gasping for breath.

There was silence in the room for a minute; then Maurice lifted up his voice and burst into loud weeping.

"Hush you, now," said Louisa. "It's only an old rabbit. It's not right to take on so."

But Maurice would not be quiet, and the noise of his weeping in the sunny nursery that morning, round the untouched breakfast, seemed the presage of disaster.

"I shall never see him again," he wailed between his sobs. "Not till we meet in Heaven."

When they told their mother she was very sorry. She suggested that they should have a proper funeral, and lent them a handkerchief with a broad black border, which she had worn at her own grandfather's funeral when she was a little girl.

While Dick went to dig a grave behind the nutbushes, they took Robert, the wooden horse, with his cart to the rabbit-hutch and laid poor Jack Baba tenderly in the cart, which he exactly fitted. Then they covered him with the black-and-white handkerchief and laid on top of that a white rose which Delia had picked from her own tree. They pulled Jack Baba all the way from his hutch to the grave. Maurice walked in front, since the horse and cart were his property, and Delia came behind, guiding the cart round the corners. Lucy and Miriam followed: Lucy played tunes on a comb—all the saddest tunes she knew—and Miriam held a bunch of mignonette and some of Jack Baba's favourite radishes.

When they came to the place where the path dips downhill, the procession was dificult to manage, for the cart, being the heavier, went faster than Robert and several times nearly upset. Dick had dug the grave under the hedge and, after Delia had lined it with moss, they buried Jack Baba with the rose, the radishes and the mignonette. But the black-and-white handkerchief was returned to their mother, to keep for another occasion. By this time they were all quite cheerful, particularly Maurice, because Dick had promised to give him a young owl which he had found in the loft. Maurice could hardly wait for the funeral to be over.

"Troubles never come singly," said Louisa. No sooner had they buried Jack Baba than they found a dead field-mouse on the lawn and a dead rook on the back drive. Then, next day, the dogs chased and killed a baby squirrel before Delia could rescue it. It seemed a worse tragedy than Jack Baba's death, and Delia was inconsolable. Lucy decided to write a grand Funeral Service. Meantime, they laid the bodies of the rook, the squirrel and the field-mouse on the sloping roof of the saddle-room, where the dogs could not get them.

Lucy told David about the proposed Funeral Service that

same day, when they had finished their Latin lesson with Mr. Vaughan and rushed out to play in the garden.

"Animals haven't souls, so they can't have proper services," said David.

"How d'you know they haven't souls?" asked Lucy. "Anyway," she added, before David could reply, "Delia has thought of a way out. She says she won't be happy in Heaven without dogs and rabbits, and she'll tell God so, and then He'll simply have to give them souls, because it would be no use being in Heaven if you weren't happy."

"I think Heaven will be full of rivers," said David, ``and everyone will have a boat of his own. How do you imagine it?"

"I'm not sure," said Lucy slowly. "It keeps changing. But I should like to slide down moonbeams on to clouds. I used to think the silliest things when I was small."

"What kind of things?"

Lucy hesitated. "Well, you know, years ago I used to long to wear a black dress and white frilly apron and cap, like Sarah, and I thought that everyone in Heaven —Jesus and the angels and all—went to bed in a long room, and in the early morning I would get up, very quietly, and put on my cap and apron and cook the breakfast and make the coffee. Then when Jesus woke up He would be very surprised and pleased, and say: 'Well done, thou good and faithful servant!' "

"What a silly idea!" said David scornfully.

Lucy was sorry that she had told him.

"Let's invent the Funeral Service," she said, in order to change the subject.

David agreed. "But I don't think it ought to be about God and Jesus," he added.

Lucy fetched an old exercise-book and a pencil, and they ran to their favourite place, under a sprawling apple tree beside the river. There, between them, they wrote a liturgy, to be used on all occasions by dogs, rabbits, mice and other animals, including toys, and particularly, said David, toy soldiers. It began quite cheerfully:

> "O to the dog of dogs,
> O to the rabbit of rabbits,
> Let us pray and to the septer of the king of the sea.
> Rex!
> Omnes veri Regem et Reginam amant.
> Praise ye the King of rabbits and the King of dogs
>   and the queen of rats and the prince of mice.
> Regina!
> Praise ye them and glorify them.
> O ye children of men, honour them and serve them.
> In the name of the queen of the fairies and the
>   king of rabbits.

ARMEN.

> O dog of dogs, have mercy upon us siners,
> Be good to us, O King, and make us joyful;
> Save us all from breaking and illness,
>   O King of the princes of dogs, and bless the
>   holy one here present, and save our King,
> O King of dogs.

> Praise o praise our doggy king,
> Praise him through this long dark night
> With the joy of sweet daylight,
> Through the holy dog of dogs.

ARMEN.

Now comes more war that we may use the valour we have got, and we pray that we fight like the men of days gone by, many of them dead. In the name of the queen of the fairies and the king of the rabbits.

ARMEN.

Many of the battles we cannot remember, as most of the most brave are dead now, but there are a few remaining; but if we only acted as they do, if we die is it not something to be read about in this book, and recorded for ever in the mind of the holy dog?"

"That will do for a beginning," said David, as Lucy finished inscribing this. "We'll think of the last bit, to say round the grave, later. Let's go and find the others."

They ran back through the orchard and, as they climbed the bank, there came to Lucy's ears the loveliest music she had ever heard. It was better than the gramophone records of "Rigoletto " and "Mignon"; better than Shân playing the piano, or the tunes her father drew so sweetly from his fiddle, when he tucked it under his chin and played to the children in the evening. This was different music: it came from everywhere, and yet from nowhere; it was like the wind and the rain, and at the same time it came from inside Lucy's own head, so that she knew that this was the music for which she had always been waiting.

"Come on," shouted David, breasting the bank. "There's someone playing a harp. Hurry up."

So, after all, it was a harp! Why had she imagined anything else? A grey-haired man was playing it on the lawn before the house, while everyone stood round listening.

"It's John Roberts!" said David.

The harpist, who was sitting with his back to them, turned at the words. When he saw David and Lucy, he swept his hands once more over the strings and broke into "Jenny Jones," and afterwards into "Hunting the Hare" and "Hob-y-deri-dando." At that they all fell to dancing—David, Delia, Lucy, Maurice and Miriam, each to himself or herself, gravely and joyfully, and their mother and the maids and Dick (who had been hiding in the bushes) clapped and laughed, for no one in all Wales could play the harp so well as John Roberts.

From merry tunes he turned to sad ones—"Bugeilio'r Gwenith Gwyn," and "David of the White Rock." The music was desolate, and now Lucy knew what was in all their hearts when Jack Baba died. She thought, "I shall write a funeral hymn, the saddest and most beautiful that ever was written."

When he had finished, John Roberts rose from his seat and said:

"You have heard me. Now you shall hear the heavenly music," and he turned his harp a little toward the south-west, so that they heard a faint sighing in the strings as the breeze swept through them and passed on its way. Even the winds made music for Roberts the Harpist.

His visit was so exciting that the children forgot about the funeral of the rook, the squirrel and the mouse. Next day Delia remembered them and hurried to the stable yard, but they had vanished. When she asked Beedles if he had seen them he said he did not hold with "dead varmint," and had thrown them away.

Lucy lost the exercise-book in which she and David had written the liturgy; it was not found again until long afterwards.

Chapter Twelve

The Birthday

Lucy was lying on the lawn under the sycamore, an exercise-book in front of her and a piece of cotton hanging out of her mouth. The other end of the cotton was fastened to a loose tooth and had been like that for two days, since she lacked the courage to do any of the things which were constantly urged on her by others— either to pull it herself, or to let someone else pull it, or to fasten the cotton to a door-handle and then slam the door. And now she had come into the garden to write poetry, partly in order to stop thinking about the tooth, but also driven by the thought of her mother's approaching birthday, since she had vowed to give her an album entirely filled with original verses.

The birthday was drawing near, only a few of the pages were filled, and Lucy gnawed her pencil. At first the shade of the sycamore had seemed perfection, but now that she was there she began to wonder if it was, after all, really such a good place for writing poeery. There were so many things to look at, to hear and to smell. Then she noticed a brilliant green caterpillar wriggling its way towards her over the grass, and immediately an idea for a poem came into her head. She seized her pencil and began to write.

THE CATERPILLAR

Caterpillar, Caterpillar, how short are thy legs;
I suppose you are the butterfly's tiny little eggs.
Caterpillar, Caterpillar, how nicely you are green,
You're quite a sight on this lawn to be seen.

So far, so good, but you couldn't have a whole poem about a caterpillar. Lucy cast about in her mind and remembered the hedgehog who had tied himself up in the tennis-net the night before and been liberated by Delia a desperately tangled ball, his brown spikes wet with dew—in the early morning. So she went on:

> Caterpillar, Caterpillar, how sweetly you can stretch,
> Every other creature is such a silly wretch.
> Now then, like the hedgehog,
> That round and prickly goose,
> If only he could stretch himself
> He'd be of far more use.

The words "Now then" did not greatly please her, but there seemed no other way of introducing the hedgehog.

She had just finished this when she saw Delia coming across the lawn, carrying her work-basket.

"Delia, Delia, come quick," she called. "I've written another poem."

Delia sat down and spread out her sewing things. She was embroidering a holland table cloth with pink and yellow daisies for her mother's birthday.

"I'll listen if you like," she said obligingly.

Lucy read the poem aloud: it did not seem so successful now as she had thought at first.

"It's not one of my particularly good ones, but it fills up the book a bit," she said apologetically.

"I like the line about the butterfly's eggs," said Delia. "Which d'you call your particularly good ones?"

"Napoleon," replied Lucy promptly. "I'll read it to you again," and, turning the pages, she began hurriedly before Delia could say anything.

Napoleon noted of all fame,
Napolcon Bonaparte by name,
Who greatly conquered all
From Russia's snowy height
To the sunny slopes of Gaul.
Like a bird who rises high away
Brought down by gun that very same day,
For when from Waterloo
He thus was caused to run,
Ringing in his ears
The warlike sound of gun,
When he sat on St. Helena
Brooding the hours by,
Wishing perhaps very often
That he might quickly die
To rise to that higher land
Never to be taken Captive by England.
So Napoleon ended his great days
On St. Helena,
Frowning on the sea
With a steadfast gaze.

"It's rather grand," Delia said at the end. "Only you don't really say what Napoleon did, do you?"

"I do," said Lucy indignantly. "I go on saying what he did the whole time. Listen!"

"No, don't start again," said Delia hastily. "I don't quite know how to explain, but it's as if you said:

'That man over there; that man you see walking on the hill; that man with a dog; that man with a hat on his head'— and then stopped."

"It's not like that in the least," said Lucy hotly. "I've mentioned almost everything that ever happened to Napoleon—Russia and Waterloo and St. Helena and even his death and the world to come. You couldn't ask for more than that in one poem."

Delia gave it up.

"What others have you?" she asked, re-threading her needle.

"Well, there's the birthday one for Mum, which goes first in the book, with a border of flowers all round. It's called 'To my Mother':

> With hair so fair,
> With eyes so blue,
> With face so true,
> With lips that speak the kindest words,
> With voice that sounds just like the birds,
> With silky dress so soft and thin
> And in her heart is not a sin.

"Then I've written one for Daddy too."

"But it isn't his birthday." Delia was quite shocked. "You shouldn't do that, you know."

"I know, but I thought he might feel left out, with no birthday till next March, and, anyway, I've written it. It's quite short:

> Tall as an arrow,
> Straight as a dart;
> With flashing blue eyes
> And such a kind heart,
> This is my father,
> The creme-de-la-creme,
> And if I adore him
> Then who is to blame?"

"Can you call people 'creme-de-la-creme'?" Delia asked dubiously. "What does it mean exactly?"

"It means the topmost top, which is just what I want it to mean," said Lucy firmly.

"Well now, about the entertainment," said Delia, changing the subject. "How are you getting on with Lady Isabelle?"

"Not very fast," sighed Lucy, on whom the duties of family Laureate sometimes weighed heavily. "It's all in my head, but it takes so long to write out, and I lost the exercise-book I was writing it in; but Louisa found it this morning behind the bathroom cupboard, so now I can go on again."

"Shan comes to-morrow and then we can start rehearsing," said Delia, and added, "There's Louisa with the bathing towels. Come on!"

Louisa was already undressing the little ones on the bank when they reached the river. Delia and Lucy, in the absence of grown-ups, occupied the tent, emerging from its discreet and canvas-scented gloom every few minutes to drive away the pigs, who were full of ungentlemanly curiosity.

Maurice, wearing nothing at all but a straw hat, pranced outside the door:

"Look at Lucy, with cotton hanging out of her mouth!" he chanted. "Cowardy, cowardy custard!"

"I'm not a coward. Get out, Snowdrop!" cried Lucy; beating the white pig with the back of her shoe. "If I wanted to pull out my tooth I should do so."

"Then why don't you?"

"Because it helps me to think of poetry. I just pull the cotton and it gives me an idea. You couldn't write poetry if you had a piece of cotton hanging from every tooth in your head."

"I don't want to, thank you," said Maurice loftily. "Poets are a silly set."

"Stop squabbling and put on your bathing drawers," ordered Louisa. "And don't go in the water, Lucy, till I've fastened up your hair."

The river, with its golden lights and brown shadows, its

scurrying minnows that fled like ghosts from your bare feet, had a way of settling quarrels and smoothing the most vexatious problems. Floating on her back with the sun on her face, Lucy thought: "What I said to Maurice about the tooth giving me ideas wasn't a bit true. Perhaps I'd better tell him so.

She turned over and swam slowly back towards the bank. Delia and Maurice were playing leap-frog with each other, and Miriam, on a pair of pink inflated wings, her yellow curls streaming, beat the water like a dog, while Louisa shouted warnings and admonitions from the bank. At Lucy's approach Maurice flung himself on his back and kicked up fountains of water in Lucy's face, but she came on towards him shouting:

"Listen, Maurice, I'll let you life-save me if you like."

The bombardment ceased and Maurice's feet went down to the bottom.

"Do you really mean that?" he asked.

"Just once," said Lucy. "Only promise not to kick."

Attempts at "life-saving" were a favourite pastime of the three eldest children, but all of them hated being the "corpse." Lucy chose this ordeal as a form of penance which would do, she felt, instead of confession, and Maurice accepted it handsomely. He even went further.

"If you like," he said, when Lucy had come up spluttering from the bottom, "you can say some of your poetry to me. I don't mind listening."

"I'll read it to you after lunch in the Tree House," said Lucy. "Watch me swimming with only my legs—Oh, Louisa, must we come in yet?"

Dressing in the pleasant stillness of the tent, Delia was suddenly inspired: "What about a prologue before 'Lady Isabelle'?"

"Who's to write the prologue?" asked Lucy cautiously, removing a holly leaf from her bare toes.

"Both of us," said Delia. "We'll be two water nymphs

who've come out of the river to salute a mortal on her birthday. Don't you think it's a good idea?"

Lucy sat down on the grass outside the tent door and shook out her hair in the sun. She and Delia were alone, for Louisa had wrung out the bathing clothes and taken the two youngest—dressed and dry—back to the house. Lucy felt extraordinarily happy, with the new-born bliss of one who has written a poem, however bad, and bathed in a fresh and lovely river on a summer day.

"Yes, it's quite a good idea," she said lazily, watching with half-closed eyes a brilliant, gauzy dragon-fly hovering over the river.

"But I think that if I were a water nymph I should stay there. I wouldn't come out at all, not even for a birthday—Oh, Delia, something's happened!"

"Have you thought of another poem," asked Delia from the back of the tent.

"No, it's my tooth. It's come out all by itself, and it isn't even bleeding!"

Shân came next day and rehearsals began in earnest for "Lady Isabelle." They rehearsed in the garden, and at Crying Corner, the strip of orchard by the ford where the water, running over the stones, kept up a continual murmuring comment, and the dippers flashed in the sunshine from rock to rock. Delia played Lord Edward; Lucy, of course, was Lady Isabelle, and Maurice doubled the parts of Lord Edward's squire and Lady Isabelle's page-boy.

Dick, the stable-boy, was alternately a lonely shepherd and the whole of the besieging army, receiving boiling oil on his head, while Shân was cast for the part of the Spanish Don, and forgot her words afresh every time.

"I don't believe Shân even tries to remember," said Lucy despairingly. But Delia was more charitable.

"It isn't really her fault. Grown-ups are like that;

something happens to their brains so that they simply don't remember the important things."

"That's what they call decay, I suppose," Lucy pondered. "It's funny. I simply can't forget things; not only poetry, but the names of all Louisa's brothers and sisters, and the maids' birthdays, and every book I've read in my life. I just can't forget."

"What about your multiplication tables?" asked Delia.

"Oh, well, they're different. No one could be expected to remember anything so dull."

At last the birthday dawned. The dogs all wore ribbons on their collars, and the breakfast table was loaded with presents. Delia's table-cloth, carefully ironed by Louisa, was greatly admired; but the children's mother loved all their gifts, from Maurice's satin pin-cushion, which was grey rather than white, to Lucy's album of verse with its border of smudged flowers round the Birthday Ode. She declared they were the best possible presents.

The play was to be performed after tea, which was spread under the beech trees on the lawn. Delia was pale with anxiety and could hardly eat any of the birthday cake, which Shân had decorated with pinks and sweet-peas. Lucy felt excited and a little frightened.

It is well known that a bad dress-rehearsal means a good first night, but Delia and Lucy were too inexperienced to know this. The last rehearsal in the garden on the previous day had gone disastrously. Shân remembered nothing at all except the Spanish oath "Carumba!"; Maurice rushed on with the words: "My Lady, Lord Edward approaches!", when Lord Edward was already on the stage making love to Lady Isabelle, and as the lonely shepherd Dick did nothing but snigger and mumble his words.

"It's bein' all alone saying them words that fair gets me,"

he said apologetically, when at last author and producer had lost their tempers.

"Well, he needn't be all alone," said Lucy. "Maurice can be another shepherd. There'll be time for him to change his clothes."

"But Maurice mustn't have any more lines to learn," said Delia firmly. "I've had trouble enough to teach him already, and he'll only get them mixed."

"Let them sing together, then," said Lucy. "That'll do nicely, and I'll come on and ask: 'Kind Shepherds, what sing ye?' instead of 'Kind Shepherd, what dost thou?'"

The rest of the company voted this a good idea, although a difficulty arose when it was found that the only tunes Dick and Maurice knew in common were hymn-tunes. After much discussion they chose "Hushed was the evening hymn," as being the least unsuitable, although the many verses referring to Samuel's heart and Samuel's ear, etc., held up the action of the play.

"For goodness' sake, don't sing more than one verse, and be less lugubrious about it," said Shân, with some irritation, when the two shepherds had slowed reverently to an end.

These last-minute changes naturally filled both Delia and Lucy with apprehension; yet in the end it proved groundless. Waiting breathlessly behind the screen which Louisa was to move back at a given signal, the two water-nymphs heard the audience enter the room—their father and mother, obviously on tiptoe with excitement; then the second row—Mrs. Bannister, Sarah, Bessie and Jane, and, clumping in behind them, Beedles, Jarman and Davey John. As Dick's father, Beedles was sharing a little of the actors' anxiety.

Delia nodded, Louisa swept back the screen, and the two nymphs, draped in shawls, scarves and Shân's green motoring veil, allowed the applause to die down.

Then they began, steadily enough:

> We are Water-Nymphs from the crystal stream,
> In the caverns dark and deep, there we lie and dream;
> In the river cool and deep,
> There we lie and swim and sleep.

First Nymph:

> Oh, love you not the river swift and free?

Second Nymph:

> Ah, but the land has fairer charms for me.
> I love the yellow fields of corn
> That stretch toward the rosy morn,
> And in the grass so fresh and green
> So many a beauteous sight is seen.

And a great deal more in the same strain.

The poem was conscientious rather than inspired, and both Delia and Lucy had been heartily sick of the subject before they had finished compiling it on their beds in the early morning. At the time it had seemed inordinately long, and very moving—like "The Forsaken Merman"—but now, on this great occasion, to which they had looked forward so eagerly, the arduously composed lines sped by with surprising speed. Scarcely had they grown accustomed to the sound of their voices in the silent room before the recitation was finished, and the water-nymphs were bowing to the human audience, while Louisa stood by with the screen.

Then they rushed away to change into Lord Edward and Lady Isabelle.

As Lord Edward, Delia wore trunken hose, a cloak made out of a curtain, and a pink pie-frill round her chin. Lucy had a cherry-coloured silk petticoat, a muslin bodice of her grandmother's and a wreath of artificial roses on her head, as became so romantically minded a heroine. For a minute or two she was nervous, and the famous parting scene with Lord

Edward— beginning, "Alas, my Lord, and must thou go so soon? Scarce have our wedding bells ceased their sweet chime when thou art called forth to this cruel war," which had been acted so often as a monologue on the back landing— lacked some of its usual gusto. But gradually confidence returned. Before the end of the first scene Lucy had ceased to be someone dressed up in other people's clothes. She was a beautiful, unfortunate lady whose husband had gone to the war. Alone in her solitary tower, wringing her hands and bewailing her lot, she thought to herself, "This is so sad that I am nearly crying; I wish I could make Davey John cry too." But he was not near enough for her to see if she had succeeded.

The next scene disclosed a glade in the forest and the two shepherds (Maurice a little breathless from his quick change of clothes) singing the first verse of "Hushed was the evening hymn," which they did so plaintively that Mrs. Bannister was seen to wipe her eyes.

The third and last scene was by far the most exciting. By this time the castle was besieged by the Spanish Don, and Louisa and Dick were kept busy off stage dropping croquet balls or banging tin trays to represent the bombardment. They did this with such good-will that many of Lady Isabelle's affecting speeches were lost in the noise. Maurice rushed on and cried: "Fly, my Lady, e'er it be too late!" and immediately afterwards Dick appeared, carrying the lid of the boiler for a shield, and marching round and round to show that he was an entire army.

But the best moment of all was Shân's entry as the villainous Don. She wore knickerbockers of green art muslin and a peacock's feather in her hat. The audience roared with excitement and joy, and seemed not to care in the least whether or not she remembered her words. Even "Carumba" was lost in the applause, and when Lord Edward and the Don fought a duel and the Don fell to the ground and Lord Edward and Lady Isabelle were united in each other's arms the noise was terrific. Davey John stood up and waved. Mrs. Bannister threw her apron over her face, and the children's parents laughed till the tears ran down their cheeks.

Then Louisa rushed forward with the screen while the Don got up from the ground and straightened his pie-frill.

So it was all over, the entertainment which they had planned for so long and with such ardour. It was finished — the story of Lady Isabelle which had been Lucy's private drama, and she wondered if she would ever play it again on the back stairs now that its tears, its passions and its pathos had been exposed to the public. And the public had laughed! They had sat solemnly enough through the first scenes, but that last one, on which Lucy had lavished her best writing, had filled them with merriment; her own speeches had been lost in Louisa's and Dick's ill-timed noises behind the scenes, and Shân, who had made no effort at all to study her part, had brought down the house by merely wearing green muslin knickerbockers and fighting a duel. Of what use was it to write a play?

Standing by Delia's side on the stage these thoughts sped through Lucy's mind then she became aware that someone was crying "Author!" It was called again: "Author! author!", mixed with shouts of "Miss Lucy!" from the men at the back.

"We want the author!" she heard her father's voice say firmly, and at the same moment Shân pushed her forward in front of the screen. She stood there for a minute while they all clapped, and her father solemnly presented her with a bunch of flowers which he had plucked from a vase; then something suddenly snapped inside her, her eyes filled with tears and she rushed into her mother's arms, the wreath of paper roses fallen down over her face.

"I didn't mean it to be funny. I meant it to be sad," she sobbed. "But you did think it a little bit sad, didn't you?"

Her mother hugged her tight.

"Darling Lucy," she said. "I think it was the saddest, loveliest play I've ever seen, and it was just too clever of you to write it."

"Delia helped an awful lot," Lucy said in a muffled voice, drying her eyes on the cherry-coloured petticoat.

"Of course she did," said her mother. "Where should we all be without Delia? And as for Maurice, I'd no idea he was such an actor."

"And Dick too," said Delia.

"And Dick too. Everyone was splendid. And now what do you all say to a dance to finish the evening? Someone turn on the gramophone, and afterwards we'll have the most delicious refreshments."

"Yes, yes," they cried and ran to wind up the gramophone. Then they all danced—Lord Edward and the Spanish Don, Maurice and Louisa, Dick and Bessie, and Lady Isabelle with her father because he said she was the "leading lady." Lucy wasn't sure what that was exactly, but she straightened her wreath, flung the cherry silk petticoat over her arm and pranced lightly round the room. In the end it had all come right. Long ago Lady Isabelle had been nothing but a phantom of her mind. Now everyone knew her; she was real, she was alive, and she, Lucy, had been hailed as "Author."

Chapter Thirteen

Blackberries and Mushrooms

The first partridge shoot of the year took place at a farm called Camlad, which lay in the hills and belonged to Mr. Gwyn. This provided the best excuse in the world for a picnic, and Delia and Lucy woke up delightedly to see a white mist outside the window which heralded a fine September day. No one loved a picnic so much as their mother, so it was sad that she could not join them, for Grandmother was coming to stay and she had chosen that very day to arrive at Pengarth.

"Of course I must be here to welcome her," said Mrs. Gwyn, "but there is no reason why Delia and Lucy should not go without me. They are quite old enough to look after their father and see that the men have plenty to eat. Beedles can drive them up in the dog-cart."

Delia and Lucy felt very important and responsible when the lunch baskets were carried down the yard and stowed into the bottom of the trap. Delia sat in front beside Beedles and Lucy perched on the back seat, with her legs swinging over the baskets.

"Mind you don't give them bottles a kick, Miss Lucy," said Mrs. Bannister. "Don't forget the salad-dressing," she told Delia. "I've put the lettuce in a cloth and there's plenty of cheese for the men."

They set off down the drive, waving and blowing kisses to their mother, and Lucy was torn between sorrow at leaving her behind and thinking how jolly it was to be going on a picnic, and how much better than eating Irish stew and rice pudding in the dining-room. When they left the high-road and turned into the lane Delia persuaded Beedles to let her drive Fancy, who was, as Beedles remarked, "full of grass" and in no mood to go briskly. The lane was strewn with loose stones and dipped in and out of hollows which had been running water-courses all the winter months. Lucy clung to the seat to keep herself from falling out. The hazel branches brushed their heads as they passed by, and Beedles pulled down a cluster of nuts and tossed them into Lucy's lap. She cracked them with her teeth, but the white kernels were not yet fully grown. When they came to the top of the lane and turned on to the hill road—which is broad and well made—Beedles took the reins from Delia and shook Fancy into a trot.

The air was lighter here after the green closeness of the lane. With the valley at their feet and Pengarth chimneys smoking in the trees, Lucy thought what a fine thing it was to be sitting up in the back of the tall dog-cart, so high that she could see over the hedges while the dusty road—like a white ribbon—ran out from under her feet. She swung her legs to and fro, humming softly to herself, and kicked over one of the baskets, whereupon she remembered Mrs. Bannister's warning and sat still. In front, Beedles was telling Delia how to treat a horse for the colic.

"Give him a drench of good hot ale, with ginger in it, and then walk him up and down . . . it all comes, I tell 'ee, from letting a hoss drink when he's sweatin'. Now, old Sir John Pryse-Powell, he had a groom . . ."

But at this point Lucy ceased listening and began to imagine herself riding over the hills on a white pony, wearing a green jacket, with a feathered hat on her head, and carrying a falcon on her wrist.

"What a smell there is of cider!" said Delia suddenly.

"What's that? Cider, d'you say?" asked Beedles.

Lucy came out of her dream.

"I think it's rather a nice smell," she said lazily.

"I'd best see if them bottles is all right," said Beedles. He pulled up Fancy, handed the reins to Delia and jumped down.

"Bless my soul!" he exclaimed when he had come round to

the back. "The cider's all run out under your feet, Miss Lucy. And you a-settin' there and saying nothing!"

"There's a trail of it along the road like a watercart," said Delia.

"The bottle's cracked, that's what it is." Beedles's head was under the seat. "There's a waste of good stuff! It's lucky that Mrs. Bannister put in a couple of them. D'you think you kicked it over, Miss Lucy?"

"I did hear a sort of a noise," said Lucy in a small volce.

"Well, it beats me how you never noticed it," said Beedles. "And the cider running out like a tap!"

The farm called Camlad lay hidden in a cup of the hills with fields of yellow stubble and little upland pastures, blue with devil's-bit scabious, on every side. There was a green duck-pond in the middle of the yard, a mountain-ash tree beside the door, and a row of pigsties—big enough to house a herd—before the parlour window. Beyond the house was a steep dingle where foxes and badgers had their holes and where the best blackberries in the countryside grew at this time of year.

Mrs. Gethin, the farmer's wife, came out to welcome the children in her snowy apron, with a silver brooch at her throat on which the word "Mother" was inscribed. Lucy thought this a beautiful idea. While Beedles unharnessed Fancy in the farmyard, Mrs. Gethin took Delia and Lucy into the best kitchen, which had a red brick floor, a shining oak tallboy with brass handles, and a row of painted flower-pots filled with geraniums on the window-sill. On the wall was a sampler with the alphabet and the words: "Martha Jane Gethin. Fear the Lord. 1874." worked in cross-stitch. Near the window was a coloured print of Daniel in the den of lions which Delia and Lucy studied with great interest. Except that Daniel was completely bald he and the lions looked much alike, with the same long beards and mild expressions.

"He doesn't look really frightened, does he," whispered Lucy.

"Of course not," said Delia with decision. "He knows that God will help him."

"But I think I should have been just a little frightened," objected Lucy.

Meanwhile, Mrs. Gethin had spread a white cloth on the table and laid out her rosy-patterned plates while Delia and Lucy unpacked the baskets. There was cold meat, a fresh loaf, butter and cheese, one of Mrs. Bannister's currant cakes, cool lettuce, and yellow plums from the garden wall. Delia put aside a just portion of these things for Twm and Beedles, who ate their dinner in the Gethins' big kitchen, and the remaining bottle of cider was honourably divided in two. Then, just as they had finished their preparations and were feeling almost too hungry to wait any longer, they saw their father with Captain Beddoes (who had come over from Cwm to shoot) and Twm the Weeg, in his cloth gaiters, with their guns and dogs, come into the farmyard. Mr. Gethin was there too, wearing a "dickie" which he had a habit of removing and leaving on a hedge when he felt the heat.

Captain Beddoes was a tall man with bright blue eyes and a bushy moustache. He had an abrupt way of asking questions and a loud laugh which terrified Lucy. If she was silent he was sure to ask her a question so loudly and clearly that everyone in the room heard and listened for the reply; and if—hoping to avoid the question—Lucy ventured on a remark of her own, he was certain to greet it with a roar of laughter. When he tramped into the room at Camlad in his heavy shooting-boots, Lucy wished that she were invisible, or at least so small that she could hide in one of the geranium pots. But when their father came in and kissed Delia and swung Lucy up in his arms, telling them both how clever they had been to arrange everything so nicely, then it was all right, although Delia had really done all the arranging and Lucy still felt a little unhappy about the cider.

They sat down to lunch, and all the things from home tasted different, eaten in that room, and on Mrs. Gethin's rosy china—as different as eggs and marmalade do when eaten for tea. Lucy began to imagine how it would be if they lived always at Camlad. She and Delia would get up very early in the morning and drive the cows in from the hill; she would have a little three-legged milking-stool of her own, and on Tuesdays she would drive to town with Mr. Gethin in his bowler hat and stand in the market hall behind a stall, wearing black buttoned boots like Jenny Gethin, and sell butter and cheeses and chickens and baskets of whinberries and white goose wings . . .

Captain Beddoes's voice broke into her dream:

"Let's ask Lucy. She's still in the schoolroom. What do you say, eh, Lucy?"

Lucy had no notion of what he was talking, and the word "schoolroom" threw her into a panic. Was he about to ask her a question in arithmetic, or the capital of Portugal, or the date of the battle of Sedgemoor? Arithmetic would be the worst; at the mere thought of a sum her mind grew blank and black. Outside the window she could see Mrs. Gethin's ducks going by to the pond, wiggle-waggle, one behind the other. Ducks were never asked questions by men with fierce moustaches, or told they had not been attending.

"Why, I believe she was up in the clouds all the time," said the Captain with a gust of laughter. "A penny for her thoughts, eh, Delia?"

Lucy's father put one of his hands over hers.

"Tell him to keep his pennies, Lucinda. We won't tell him anything, will we,"

Lucy lifted her head and smiled into her father's merry eyes. She felt brave again, and thought the Captain's moustaches and loud voice quite stupid.

After lunch, when Mr. Gwyn and Captain Beddoes were sitting smoking in the high settle, Lucy slipped into the big kitchen with a dish of yellow plums. Mr. Gethin was telling Beedles about the fox which had stolen two of his young turkeys that week.

"An old dog-fox it was, with a white tip to his tail. He tuk them in broad daylight, and Her" (pointing to Mrs. Gethin) "did see un go out of window."

"Just like Old Mother Slipper-Slopper," thought Lucy.

"Well, you tell Dan to bring the hounds up here when they start cubbing, and we'll be having a bit of a hunt, won't we, Miss Lucy?" said Twm. He winked at the others when he said this, for the Camlad foxes were famous. No one had ever seen so many or such big ones as Mr. Gethin, though they were not always to be found when Dan the huntsman, with his hounds, came to draw the dingle.

Then it was time for the shooters to set out once more, and the dogs, wild with joy, were released from the dark stable: Bell and Juno, the two setters, old Sam, the retriever, and Twm's spaniel Dash, who was going grey about the nose but still knew his job. The men shouldered their guns and trooped out of the yard, through the top gate beyond the hayricks. Delia stood and waved, but Lucy hid behind the dairy door for fear Captain Beddoes should kiss her good-bye.

"Now we'll pick blackberries," said Delia. "Jenny says she'll show us the best places."

Jenny Gethin was a big girl—a great deal older than Delia and Lucy—with cheeks like red apples. She brought a tin can for the blackberries and Delia and Lucy each carried one of the lunch baskets. They crossed the stream over a fallen tree, ran down the sloping field and through a hunting wicket into the dingle. Here, at first, the trees stood far apart, growing on either side of the green rides, but further on there was a tangle of undergrowth where the finest blackberries grew. Jenny went straight to the largest bush and picked so hard and so fast that her can was soon more than half full. Delia plunged bravely into the middle of the thickest and thorniest bramble patch, and Lucy ran round the edges, picking all the biggest and juiciest berries and avoiding the ones that were small or difficult to reach.

Presently she and Jenny found themselves at the same bush, which was an opportunity for conversation. Lucy wasted no time.

"Jenny, which would you rather be," she asked, "dazzlingly beautiful, brilliantly clever, or angelically good?"

It was a question of their own invention which had often troubled Delia and Lucy. Both of them felt that the right answer should be "angelically good," while both of them secretly longed to choose "dazzlingly beautiful." But Jenny did not answer; she merely giggled and went on picking. Lucy shifted her ground.

"Suppose a fairy suddenly flew out of this bush and gave you three wishes—anything you liked—what would you choose?"

Jenny opened her round mouth and Lucy waited expectantly.

"The old dog-fox came out of bramble patch," she said suddenly. "Dad see'd un go—a great big un, and he ran all the way to the gorsty field on the Weeg lump."

Lucy stamped her foot.

"I'm sick and tired of hearing about foxes. People pretend they're so exciting, but they're no more interesting than cats, and I'm sure they're not half as clever."

This, she knew, was heresy, but she felt contrary, and with that she ran away down the dingle.

"There's a big old bog in the bottom," Jenny shouted after her.

Lucy ran on.

"Lucy, we're going out at the top," she heard Delia's voice

calling, and she thought: "I won't answer. Why should I? I hate picking blackberries with Jenny."

The wood was so cool and pleasant that she soon forgot her annoyance. It was full of scents and sounds, and after a little time Lucy sat down on a fallen tree and started to count the different tiny noises in the air. There was the high note of insects, the tap-tap of a woodpecker; then nothing, nothing at all except very far away the bleat of a sheep, and quite close beside Lucy the faintest rustle that might have been a field mouse in the grass or a ripe blackberry falling through the leaves. Suddenly these sounds were shattered by the noise of a gun, and after it two more shots. The shooters must be quite near, thought Lucy. Immediately the tune of the wood was changed: the tiny noises were silenced as though they were afraid; flustered birds rose and beat their way through the branches; from far down the dingle came the harsh cry of a jay, and a cock pheasant startled Lucy by creaking and whirring upwards from almost under her feet—a gorgeous creature, glowing in the leafy sunshine.

"You've one more month to enjoy yourself, my dear," Lucy remarked aloud, feeling, when she had said this, that she had at least warned the pheasant.

Then she looked down at her basket and was ashamed to see how few berries covered the gaping bottom. If only she were grown-up, with long arms and a walking-stick and long skirts to protect her legs, she was sure she would fill her basket in no time. Yet Delia entered the biggest patches in spite of her bare legs, but then Delia was brave and steadfast, Lucy wished so much that she could be brave and steadfast too, and with that wish in her heart she walked resolutely into the middle of the stoutest blackberry bush and set herself to picking. The long brambles clung malevolently round her bare legs; the goose-grass stuck to her shoulders and the vicious thorns jabbed her fingers when she stretched for the ripest berries. But Lucy picked on. She heard another shot, farther away this time, and then the wood settled down again; only it was not quite the same; the small birds seemed shyer, and a wood-pigeon clattered uneasily in and out of the branches.

Lucy's basket was growing heavy; if she tipped up one end it looked almost full, and she thoughtfully ate the juiciest ones off the top. She pushed on and found herself suddenly in the bog of which Jenny had warned her. First her shoes sank in, then it was over her ankles, and whichever way she stepped the ground grew softer. She tried jumping from tussock to tussock—knowing that the long grass hid the dry patches—and at last she saw a fallen tree sprawling in her path which promised a dry highway. Balancing carefully she had almost reached the end when the tree, like some unkind monster, rocked, turned about, and flung her into the bog. Her basket rolled away and every precious blackberry was spilled and scattered on the ground.

Poor Lucy! She tried at first to pick them up, but they were too muddy; then she sat down on the tree and tried to pull the thorns out of her legs and fingers, but there were too many, and suddenly she decided that the thing she wanted most to do was to escape from the wood. Picking up her empty basket she ran till she came to a rickety fence half hidden by bracken and beyond it a sunny field. Sitting in the field with his back to her was a man with a yellow dog. On the ground by his side lay a sack and a bundle tied up in a red pocket-handkerchief.

The man looked round.

"Good day," he said. "What's thee crying for?"

"I'm not crying," said Lucy indignantly. "At least, only a tiny bit."

"I reckon thee's lonesome," said the man. "I'd be lonesome myself if it weren't for Nell, my little tarrier dog."

"Is that Nell?" asked Lucy, drying her eyes and glancing at the yellow dog, which, she noticed, had only one ear.

"Aye, that's Nell. She's very tender-hearted to me, but she's that fierce with varmint you wouldn't believe it."

"Why has she only one ear?" asked Lucy.

"Well, now, that was an old dog-fox as done that. But she pulled the tail off him before he was finished, she's that fierce."

"Perhaps that was the fox Mr. Gethin saw," said Lucy. Clearly foxes were the favourite topic of conversation, and she was too dispirited to suggest another one.

"I don't know nuthin' about that; but this was a tremenjus big fox," said the man. Then he added: "They're shooting here to-day, seemingly."

"Yes, that's my father and Captain Beddoes," said Lucy.

"Then thee's a daughter for Gwyn, Pengarth,"

Lucy nodded.

"What's in that bag?" she asked presently. "It's moving."

"I'll show 'ee." He opened the sack and pulled out a white ferret with pink eyes; there was another one in the bottom of the dark bag.

"I don't think I like them very much," said Lucy. "What d'you use them for?"

The man gave her a sidelong glance.

"Oonts,"[1] he said, and added after a moment's pause: "What's thee been getting in thy basket?"

"They were blackberries," said Lucy, and at the thought of her loss the foolish tears came into her eyes once more.

"Well, now, whatever is the matter?" asked the man. "Is thee feared of the ferrets?"

"No, no, it isn't that. But I spilt all my blackberries in the bog, and Delia and Jenny will think I haven't picked any at all; but I did ever so many and I'm full of thorns."

---

[1] Oonts = moles

Painting of Eiluned Lewis as a little girl
writing (artist unknown)

Eiluned Lewis as a child

Eiluned Lewis when she was
in her fifties

Eiluned's elder sister Medina Lewis (Delia in the book)
and Eiluned on a donkey outside
Glan Hafren ('Pengarth')

Painting of Glan Hafren (artist unknown)

Glan Hafren

J M Barrie playing croquet on the lawn at
Glan Hafren

J M Barrie and Michael Llewellyn Davies
playing croquet

J M Barrie on the lawn

Charades at Glan Hafren. Back row, left to right: J
M Barrie; unknown person in black shawl; Eiluned
Lewis as Boadicea; Eiluned's mother Eveline Lewis;
Medina Lewis; Eiluned's aunt Adie Lewis (Shan in
the book). Front row, left to right: Eiluned's younger
sister May (Miriam in the book); Michael Llewellyn
Davies; Nicolas Llewellyn Davies

Medina, Eiluned and Michael Llewellyn Davies

"Don't cry, Missy," said the man. "I'll give thee my mushrooms."

"There aren't any mushrooms," said Lucy through her tears.

The man was busy untying the red pocket-handkerchief. When he had undone it she saw that it was full of the most delicate, milky, silvery mushrooms, with undersides of fluted pink; big ones and little ones; round, trim buttons and others as exquisite as a fairy's parasol.

"Putt them in your basket."

"Oh no, not all of them!"

"Putt them in and say no more. Thee's welcome."

Lucy stood up and held out her hand.

"You've turned my darkness into light," she said gravely. "That's our most solemn way of saying thank you. Won't you come back to Camlad with me? I'm afraid there's no cider left because I kicked over one of the bottles, but I'm sure my father would be pleased to see you."

"That's as may be," said the man. "Thank 'ee kindly, but I reckon I'll go my own way." He picked up the wriggling sack and threw it over his shoulder. "That's your best way back, along the bottom and up the gorsty field."

"Good-bye," said Lucy. "I hope we'll meet again."

"So long," said the man.

He whistled to Nell and turned away, and Lucy, with her basket full of mushrooms, ran back to Camlad.

Mrs. Gethin, Jenny and Delia were standing by the kitchen table when Lucy slipped round the door. They were busy pouring blackberries into one big basket.

"Oh, there you are! What a mess you're in," said Delia. "Did you get many?"

"I got something better," said Lucy, displaying her basket.

"Nem-o-dear, there's sharp eyes you have to be finding all those mushrooms!" exclaimed Mrs. Gethin.

"I didn't. It was a man with a bag and a dog called Nell. But I had picked a lot of blackberries, Delia. Honestly I had."

Beedles put his head round the door.

"Time to start," he said. "I'm a-goin' to put in the mare."

"Lucy, who did pick those mushrooms?" asked Delia after they had said good-bye to Mrs. Gethin and climbed into the dog-cart.

"It was an adventure," said Lucy dreamily, her eyes fixed on the blue line of distant hills that rose and fell as they bumped over the stony lane. "And he was one of the nicest men I've ever met."

"Who was?"

"The man with the ferrets who gave me the mushrooms, of course. He was catching oonts."

"Oonts, indeed!" said Beedles with scorn. "That's a likely story! Whoever heard of catching oonts with ferrets! It was rabbits he was after, and no mistake, and I don't doubt it was Billy Bennett. D'you say he had a sack? Aye, and wires too, I warrant! The old poacher!"

"He wasn't poaching," said Lucy indignantly. "He was just sitting in a field."

"Aye, sittin' in a field on your father's land! I know him. I'm surprised at you, Miss Lucy, taking up with that ontidy man. Oonts, indeed!"

"I don't care what you say," cried Lucy. "You don't know anything at all about him. He's a splendid man, I tell you—a thousand times nicer than Captain Beddoes."

Delia's soft voice interposed:

"Anyway, he gave you the mushrooms. That was very kind of him. Oh, Beedles, please let me drive Fancy all the way home."

Chapter Fourteen

Harvest Festival

Everyone was glad when Grandmother came to stay at Pengarth. Mrs. Bannister excelled herself in the making of especially rich, yellow tea-cakes, from a recipe which Grandmother had once given her, and Jarman carried a seat to a sheltered corner under the south wall of the garden. He liked to have Grandmother sitting there, wearing her panama hat and armed with a Hy-whisk, while he stood on a ladder picking the yellow plums, the rosy Victorias, and the small, sweet greengages.

The children were no less pleased with her company. It was true that, unlike Shan, she could tell few stories of the naughty things she did in her childhood—but then it was difficult to imagine anyone so gentle and so pretty as Grandmother ever being naughty. Nor would anyone have guessed that she had travelled round the world in a sailing ship, lived in tropic lands, and once been chased by a mad dog till it was killed at her feet by the ship's carpenter with a hatchet. These adventures had passed her by, leaving no trace except a slight distrust of dogs, a taste for hot curries and an unwillingness to come boating on the river at Pengarth. Perhaps something else remained as well—a faint tang of the sea, slight as a taste of salt in the wind, or the remote murmur of a sea-shell. You noticed it in her speech, when she talked of "lashing up" a parcel—and no one ever lashed up a parcel so securely as Grandmother. Then there was her sea-chest, which stood in the attic at Pengarth, bound with brass, filled with limp muslins and camphor-scented embroideries. Most noticeable of all was the melancholy that fell upon her whenever the wind howled round the house on stormy nights.

Lucy loved to hear the storm gather itself like a wild animal to rush down the valley, buffeting the windows, so that even the heavy curtains swung in the draught and the slates outsite crashed from the roof; but Grandmother sat, straight and anxious on her chair, and looked sadly into the fire. They knew then that she was thinking of the men at sea.

When Grandmother came to stay she would say, "Come and see what I have in my pocket," and then they would, all four, gather round. The pocket, made of black silk, was worn inside her skirt, and always it held something for each of them: perhaps a thimble for Delia, a pencil for Lucy and sweets for them all. The sweets were round, flat, and made of yellow gelatine. They were known as "Grandmother's Kisses," and the children were very fond of them. Then they would all sit down together and play:

> Mingledy, mingledy, clap, clap
> How many fingers do I hold up?

It was not really an exciting game, but Grandmother had a way of saying "Mingledy, mingledy" that was irresistible, and she was most artful in concealing the number of her fingers.

After that they would beg her to recite nursery rhymes in Welsh and explain their meaning. There was one beginning, "Mamgu, mamgu, capan côch," which Delia and Luy could repeat, very nearly correctly, in Welsh. It meant:

> Granny, granny, in a red cap,
> Come with me to the pigsty.
> See the wind, see the rain,
> See the little bird over there,
> See the man in leather breeches
> Shooting the King of England's ship.[1]

Then how excellent was Grandrnother's method of

Counting Out before a game, and how superior to the ordinary "Ena, Dena, Dinah, Doh"! "One-ery, two-ery, three-ery, same"; it ran:

> Bottle of vinegar, who'll be game?
> Ex and squary,
> Virgin Mary,
> Vik, vok,
> Little stock,
> Go you out, and Go!

Lucy acquired this with care, in order to show off before the Rectory children next time they picked up sides for rounders.

When Grandmother told them stories of her childhood they saw, in their minds, a bare and treeless country, with stone walls between the fields and the sound of the sea on every side; a country where the Atlantic rollers crashed on the shore and kites of foam were carried over the fields, like white birds, on the back of the wind. But if it was harsh in winter, said Grandmother, there was no country anywhere to compare with it in early summer, when every grassy chink in the stone walls was patterned with wild flowers, and the smell of the gorse in the lanes and along the sea cliffs was like warm cocoa-nut in the air.

As for Nantgwyn, where she had grown up, nowhere in all the world were blackberries so large and sweet, nor

---

[1]Mamgu, Mamgu capan coch,
Dewch gyda fi i twlc y moch.
Gwelwch y gwynt, gwelwch y gwlaw,
Gwelwch y deryn bach man draw,
Gwelwch y dyn yn britis lledr
Yn seethu llong y brenin Lloegr.

mushrooms so delicate. Grandmother thought little of the mushrooms at Pengarth, though she often asked one of the children to help her look for them. She herself was the most persevering searcher; but then she always walked so slowly that, for her, it was comparatively easy. Lucy and Maurice would run round her in circles, assuring her that there was not a mushroom to be found in that field, and advising her to try the next one. But nothing ever hurried or disturbed Grandmother, and she would confound them by finding one in the most unlikely place.

They liked to hear her tales of Nantgwyn, and of how, on winter evenings, all the women-folk of the household—the daughters and the maids—sat spinning round the fire, while Grandmother's grandfather read aloud in Welsh. Twice a year the tailor would come to stay in the house, to make suits for the men, and after him came the shoemaker to make shoes for the family. The slippers for the ladies were made from pieces of broadcloth which the tailor had left behind from cutting out the gentlemen's suits.

In the autumn at Nantgwyn some of the bullocks were killed on the farm, salted and pickled and candles made from their fat. Grandmother could remember the strands of cotton hanging over a stick, and how she would help to dip them, time and again, into a great cauldron of hot grease, until at last they were so well coated that they had turned into candles and were stored for the winter. In those days, said Grandmother, Old Christmas Day was observed, and people would ask each other: "Which are you keeping this year—Old Christmas or New Christmas?" What a chance to say "Both!", thought Lucy, and to hang up your stocking twice over.

But the story they liked best was Grandmother's account of the corn-cutting at Nantgwyn. There was, it seemed, great rivalry between the farms to be first to finish cutting the harvest, and much ceremony over the last standing island of corn. Part of it was carried to the house to be plaited into a

little doll—called the Gwrach wh
the Harvest Home supper, and af
through, from the rafters of the
was taken to any neighbourin
finished its cutting, and the your
the fastest runner. Approachin
down the corn before the peopl
his heels, for, once caught, he
ducked in the pond.

Lucy liked to picture that scene—the young man running
swiftly over the yellow stubble, carrying a shock of corn in
his arms. But in her imagination the young man turned into a
beautiful maiden—and that maiden was herself—chosen for
her fleetness of foot, and running for her life to escape being
thrown into a bottomless pool.

They were cutting the corn in the fields round Pengarth at
this time. From morning till evening the air was filled with the
click-click of the cutting-machine. But the only ceremony that
marked the end was a chorus of shouting men and yelping
dogs, as the desperate field creatures were driven out from
their last fortress of nodding wheat or silken, silvery oats.

As soon as the corn was gathered the season of Harvest
Festivals set in, and Jarman was kept busy filling hampers for
churches and chapels with fruit and vegetables and shaggy
scarlet dahlias. After Pengarth Church there were the chapels
in town, and next day came a gentle old man with a snowy
beard, pushing a wheelbarrow. He had come to beg flowers
for the little chapel at Bwlch-hafodygog, a name which
means, in English, the Mountain-pass of the Summer
Residence of the Cuckoo.

Last of all—because it was in the hills and therefore late in
cutting its corn—came the church of Llanaeron, in which
parish lay Camlad and other farms belonging to Mr. Gwyn.

Delia and Lucy had been helping Jarman and Davey John
all morning to pick apples in the big orchard. There is nothing

s picking apples on a warm, mellow autumn day. man climbed the ladder and shook the trees so that les fell thud on the grass, or glanced rattling off the of the bucket, or even bounced on Delia's and Lucy's ads, they shouted with joy. They helped Davey John to carry them up the mossy steps to the apple-room, but the brilliant red cider-apples, and the little puckered green ones which had never been much good, and the big, juicy apples on which the wasps had begun feasting, were pushed away in a wheelbarrow and tipped out in a corner of the rick-yard. And there they would remain, through rain and sunshine, until the cider-machine, with its stained sacks and the old horse who walked round and round, came lumbering on its way through the valley.

Delia and Lucy came in regretfully to wash their hands for lunch and were told they must be ready by two o'clock to drive to Llanaeron with their father. As it was a Harvest Festival they wore their white Leg-horn hats and coats of lavender blue. The capes were piped with silk of the same colour, which had once been part of Grandmother's wedding dress.

"Like to jump out and stretch your legs?" said their father, when they came to the bottom of the first hill. He made them step down while Beauty was still walking, which he said was good practice; but Lucy jumped, instead of stepping, as she was told to do, and scraped her knee on the dog-cart step.

The afternoon was warm, and Beauty a fast walker; Lucy pulled off her hat and loitered behind. The day was so still that she could hear the ripe nuts in the hedge rustling softly from twig to twig as they dropped to the ground. She climbed the bank, trying to reach the biggest clusters; ran after a late butterfly, hovering in the sunshine; stopped to see if her knee had begun to bleed, and borrowed Delia's pocket-handkerchief to tie round it.

Their father was waiting under an oak tree at the top of the hill, and pointed with his whip to the telegraph wire as they drew near.

"The swallows will soon be gone," he said. "They're making their plans."

They saw then that the wire at that point was dark with swallows, and the air alive with their rapid, eager twittering.

Delia and Lucy climbed into the dog-cart, and away they spanked up the winding road to Llanaeron. Beauty and the trap were put up at the inn stable, and then they all three walked across to the church. The women had already gone inside, but the men were standing in the churchyard, wearing their Sunday black. Delia and Lucy saw a dozen faces they knew: Mr. Gethin and his three sons; Twm the Weeg; Mr. Jones, Pantycrasty; Abraham Williams with his glass eye; Denis, whom they had not seen since the haymaking, and Evan the Shoof, so called because his aunt had once kept the Sheaf Inn.

They went into church, which smelt like the apple-room, the potato-house and a corn-field rolled into one, and there was Davey John, who showed them into a seat in the front, with a bunch of Michaelmas daisies fastened to one end, and a window-sill at the other covered with carrots and shiny apples. Opposite them was the pulpit, where Delia spotted the Pengarth grapes and dahlias. In front of it were a small stack of wheat, several jars of honey, a basket of damsons and an enormous pumpkin. Then Abraham Williams's son, Llewelyn, who seemed, curiously, to have inherited his father's glass eye, began pulling out the stops of the harmonium and in came the clergy—Mr. Morgan, the vicar of Llanaeron, a long, thin, black man, and the two visitors: Mr. Price of Llandre, fumbling under the surplice for his spectacles, and Mr. Tudor Thomas of Llegodig, looking as round, rosy and polished as the apples on the window-sill.

They began by singing "We plough the fields and scatter"—a hymn which Delia and Lucy knew well, so that they both sang it with great enjoyment and at the tops of their voices.

The clergymen then took it in turns to do things, and it seemed to Lucy that Mr. Morgan did more than his share—which showed a lack of good manners towards his visitors. Mr. Price read the lessons, but there was hardly anything at all left for poor Mr. Thomas to do, although he did not seem to mind. Lucy wondered which of them would preach the sermon, and how they settled it beforehand. Perhaps they recited Grandmother's rhyme in the vestry—

> One-ery, two-ery, three-ery, same,
> Bottle of vinegar, who'll be game?
> Ex and squary,
> Virgin Mary . . .

Quite suitable, thought Lucy, and obviously they had done it that way, for otherwise it was Mr. Thomas's turn, and here was Mr. Price climbing up the pulpit steps, and opening the Bible very carefully between the bunches of oats and the nodding dahlias.

Mr. Price chose his text from the story of Ruth and Boaz:

> "And when she was risen up to glean, Boaz commanded his young men, saying, 'Let her glean even among the sheaves, and reproach her not. And also pull out some for her from the bundles and leave it, and let her glean, and rebuke her not.' So she gleaned in the field until even; and she beat out that she had gleaned, and it was about an ephah of barley."

Lucy was very fond of the story of Ruth and she settled down happily to listen. She had often thought what a charming man Boaz must have been, and regretted that the custom of gleaning had died out. Her father, she was sure, would have been generous in just the same way, and would have told the men to let some of the corn fall to the ground. What fun to go gleaning oneself! She and Delia, dressed in the fashion of the Illustrated Bible, would pace through the neighbours' fields and bring their sheaves home to their mother in the evening, as Ruth did to Naomi.

Here she realised that she was not attending to the sermon, and abandoned her own thoughts that she might listen to Mr. Price.

"We may read in this story a beautiful parable," he was saying. "Ruth is the Church, ever in our midst. Boaz is the righteous man who recognises his responsibilities to God and does not omit to fulfil them. Note well the form of his commands to the reapers. Had he said to them, 'Let her glean among the sheaves and reproach her not,' that would have been a simple discharge of his duty, with which many Christians to-day would rest content; but he went farther than that. He said 'Also pull out some for her from the bundles and leave it.' Here, my dear friends, is an example that we should keep steadfastly before us. The Church should not be relegated to rare occasions—to Christmas Day, Easter Day or even to a Harvest Festival; we should exert ourselves to serve it, not only giving it that which we can very well spare, but depriving ourselves that others may rejoice; pulling out, as it were, golden handfuls from the sheaves of our bounty."

Lucy felt as though she had been cheated. The thought of Ruth, wandering sadly through the stubble, had turned into a picture of Mr. Price, expecting people to come to church and to put something in the collection plate. She glanced round to see what the others were thinking of this new version of the story, but Delia was gazing with starry eyes at Mary Magdalene in the East window, and her father was taking a nap. Lucy restrained herself from looking round at Davey John and fixed her gaze on the honey-pots before her. She thought, "If David and I climbed on the roof of the saddle-room, we could run along the edge. I wouldn't dare do it alone, but, if he were there too, it would be a good place for hiding, because we could either come down the ladder outside the loft or slide down by the water-butts." She was so pleased with this idea that she forgot all about Ruth and Mr. Price.

"Hymn 382, 'Come, ye thankful people, come,' " said Mr. Morgan suddenly. Lucy and her father nodded to each other to show that this was a tune of which they both approved.

"All this world is God's own field," they sang. Lucy sang joyfully, seeing the world as a wide cornfield, bounded by a river, rimmed with hills and full of kind friends who would pull out the corn from their sheaves while she gleaned in their footsteps.

> "From Thy field wilt purge away
> All that doth offend, that day;
> And Thine angels charge at last
> In the fire the tares to cast . . ."

Lucy would have liked to have gone on singing about the corn-field; the thought of the bonfire, stoked by angelic Jarmans, was less pleasing. Perhaps, after all, she wouldn't go on the roof; Louisa had frequently said she was sick of patching her knickers.

After the service was over and they had talked to people in the churchyard, there was tea in the schoolroom, with farm bread-and-butter, home-made flat tarts, and the farmers' wives busy pouring out tea and plying everyone with food. Delia and Lucy felt shy and sat together. Delia had a silent, red-cheeked boy on her left, but Lucy was next to a stout woman in a tight black silk bodice who poured out the tea and asked: "French cream, m' dear?"

"Yes, please," said Lucy, and wondered why the woman seemed surprised. The "French cream" was in a bottle, and the woman was kept busy tipping it into the teacups. It did not look at all like cream.

Mrs. Gethin came round with a currant cake of her own baking and Lucy accepted a slice and left it on her plate. The room was hot and the roof seemed to weigh on her head. From the end of a long tunnel she could hear her father joking with Abraham Williams about the huge pumpkin he had brought to the Harvest Festival. A woman Lucy did not know pressed her to take some bread-and-butter.

"Ketch in, Miss Gwyn," she said.

Lucy thought how funny it was to be called "Miss Gwyn," but she could not eat anything. On the wall opposite was a picture of the Good Shepherd. Lucy felt very queer, but she thought:

"If I look hard at that picture I shall be all right."

Everyone was talking, and the woman with the teapot and the French cream was very red in the face, but that was no wonder, for it was hot, with so many people and all the lamps lit. French cream, thought Lucy, smelt like Mrs. Bannister's cherry brandy.

At last they came away and stepped out into the cool dusk. The sunset was fading beyond the hills as they walked back to the inn. Davey John brought Beauty out of the stable and harnessed her to the dog-cart. The people at the inn had not gathered their apples: they were dark against the sunset. Over the garden wall came a curl of blue smoke and the smell of burning leaves.

Lucy sat silent all the way home. The dog-cart swung past the dim hedges; a sickle-shaped moon rose and fell behind the branches of the trees, and the lights of cottages and farm-houses swam in the dark valley below. Her father was humming the tune of the last hymn:

> "Come then, Lord of mercy, come,
> Bid us sing thy Harvest-Home;
> Let Thy saints be gathered in,
> Free from sorrow, free from sin;
> All upon the golden floor
> Praising Thee for evermore . . ."

All of them together, thought Lucy—Grandmother, and her parents, David, Louisa and Mr. Price with his church, Ruth in the corn-field, the woman with the "French cream," and the Gwrach hanging from the rafters of the ceiling over the Harvest supper all of them "praising Thee for evermore."

When they reached home she was fast asleep.

Sing, happy child, Noel, Noel!
Bright shines Orion's sword
Where every star stands sentinel
And watchful of their Lord.

Sweetly the carol-singers speak;
They fill the firelit hall,
Singing of Mary, fair and meek,
And Jesus in the stall.

Hark, happy child, to what they say,
Lock in your heart their song,
Lest you should lose it on the way
When every road seems long.
You will recall the spiced scent
Of leaves where no winds stir
When gold and frankincense are spent
And nothing's left but myrrh.

Chapter Fifteen

Winter Evenings

Outside the nursery at Pengarth was the long passage —the best place in the world for pretending to be an engine if you were Maurice. Delia and Lucy had other uses for it. To begin with, there was the cupboard at the end from which, after they had had whooping-cough, Louisa dispensed spoonfuls of a glutinous mixture out of a tall bottle labelled "Vitali Oil." No one really liked it, but it was quite jolly to take after Lucy had devised the plan of dancing the length of the passage, chanting,

> "Yo ho for Vitali Oil,
> The oil from the crystal spring,
> As up and down the passage we dance
> And this is the song we sing.
>
> Yo ho for Vitali Oil,
> That beautiful, unctuous oil,
> It makes my very, my very, my very,
> It makes my very blood boil!"

Hypnotised by this ritual they swallowed large spoonfuls of the loathsome draught.

But the passage was the scene of other revels far gayer and more elaborate. Here they would hold a Ball, to which Delia calling herself Mr. Watkins for the occasion and looking very solemn—would come in a flowered waistcoat and request the honour of a dance with Mrs. Fitzgerald. This sprightly lady was none other than Lucy, elegant in a fawn Indian muslin of Grandmother's, edged with royal blue, of which the tunic reached to her toes, while what had once been the ``bustle'' swept the floor in a train. Waving a feather fan, and with her curls screwed up in a bunch by Delia with three of Louisa's large black hairpins (kindly lent for the evening—the perilous erection reinforced by a couple of paper flowers on wire stalks—Mrs. Fitzgerald was a fascinating partner. No wonder Mr. Watkins bowed low when he stood before her to claim a dance.

Fast and furious sped the polkas up and down the passage to the noise of the comb, played by Maurice, who, seated in front of the china cupboard, would beat upon it with his elbows—the nursery tea-service within adding a genial rattle to the tune. When the paper on the comb was too moist for further sound, and the band's elbows had grown sore, a waltz was called for, and the dancers revolved, a trifle laboriously, to the thin tinkle of "The Merry Widow" played on a musical box.

When winter evenings had closed in, a lamp stood at one end of the passage, and this lamp Louisa, being too lazy to fetch another, would carry away with her when she went to wash up the tea-things. That was the children's opportunity. At Delia's suggestion hassocks and cushions were carried out from the nursery and placed, by one of them, at intervals down the length of the passage, while the others rushed to and fro at top speed, falling violently over them in the dark.

Near the far end of the passage was a board to keep Miriam from tumbling downstairs. Delia and Lucy could remember the time when they too had been baulked by that boundary and had laid siege to it with chisel and hammer: once over that board they felt the kingdom would be theirs. But now it was no longer an obstacle; they jumped over it as they ran to and fro to the tune of "Oh, du lieber Augustin"; with their arms round each other's waists they would prance down the passage, leaping the foolish board at the words: "Alles ist hin!"

Oh, why did Louisa come back with the light? Why did it last so short a time, that quarter-of-an-hour when the passage was full of mysterious shadows —the lamp on the stairs giving a dim radiance to one end, while at the other there was the firelit, lamplit nursery when the darkness outside grew frightening?

But the minutes passed all too quickly, and Louisa returned with the lamp and told them "to pick up all that caudle." The passage is itself again—not so lengthy a passage after all; nor will the board stand for long. The certainties of childhood are left behind and there is nothing now between the children and the uncertain world.

> "Oh, du lieber Augustin,
> Alles ist hin!"

It was a fact—sad, but almost inevitable—that when on winter evenings you painted in the nursery after tea —which was the best time of day since there was no longer any possibility of being dragged out for a walk, or told to do your piano practice—then the pictures, which by lamplight had appeared so fair, wore an altered complexion next morning. Thus when Lucy had coloured, with pride and pleasure, all the illustrations in "The Rime of the Ancient Mariner," it was disconcerting to find the following day that the Ancient Mariner, instead of being "long and lank and brown as is the ribbed sea sand," was long and lank and purple, with a beard of deep crimson.

"It's because you keep your paint-box in such a mess," said Louisa, when Lucy wailed over the discovery, for the Ancient Mariner was one of her favourite characters. She had even adopted some of his language and shocked Miss Crabtree by using the word "hellish" in connection with a long-division sum.

Delia was more sympathetic over the Mariner's changed hue.

"I've often done it myself," she said kindly. "If you like I'll paint over him, only then his beard will be black instead of brown."

Delia's paint-box was beautifully tidy, and she had besides a lump of gamboge, a tube of rose madder and some real gold paint with which she adorned the haloes of the Saints in her Sunday painting book. Her brushes were of sable, and she always had a painting-rag. None of these things could be said of Lucy, who, having lost all her brushes, lived on a wretched borrowed one of Maurice's, while, although Louisa was always giving her new painting-rags, she had been known to use her pocket-handkerchief, and even her pinafore.

Yet no one could have wished more ardently than Lucy to paint beautiful pictures. The Odes which she wrote to her father and mother on their birthdays were illustrated with coloured borders and illuminations, but since they were seldom begun until the compulsion of the last moment drove her to the task, the results were often messy and disappointing. Yet it seemed that her parents treasured them in spite of their blemishes, and when her father hung up her last Ode, with its smudged pictures, on the wall of his dressing-room Lucy was filled with shame and good intentions. If only she had started it earlier it might have been better! Because he loved everything she did she longed to write him the most magnificent poems, paint him the most exquisite pictures. Something long and affecting, such as "Marmion," or "The Lady of Shalott," she fancied, with illustrations not unlike Mr. Rackham's.

Inspired by these ambitions she had begun a long narrative poem for her father on Christmas Day, and now, on Christmas Eve, she was still far from the end. Delia had finished long ago the slippers and tea-cosy which she had made for her parents; even Maurice had struggled to the completion of a cross-stitch kettle-holder and a ball of coloured shaving papers; and all these things had been made in secret, with Louisa's connivance, and hidden at the sound of their parents' approaching footsteps. But Lucy's present to her mother—a mat ornamented with ravelled French knots in which the needle had been too often and too desperately entangled—had been finished by Louisa, and the poem, with no end in sight and its first rapture long since evaporated, still trailed a meandering length.

They had spent the morning of Christmas Eve helping to hang the holly and ivy over the house, and now the nursery lamp was lit in its fresh bower of mistletoe, and on the table beneath Lucy had spread out her paint-box, a mug of water and her "Poem" on several sheets of drawing-paper; at the other side Delia was busy with scissors and paste and gold paper making golden crowns and magic wands for the New Year's Eve entertainment. Louisa, in the rocking-chair, and beside her Bessie, the housemaid, were mending stockings; Bessie was telling Louisa about her young man, who appeared mysteriously in all her stories as "They."

"I was wearing my blue costume," said Bessie, "and They come along and made personal remarks. 'Well, I never,' I said. 'There's cheeky you are, and no mistake!'"

"What are 'personal remarks,' Bessie?" Lucy interrupted.

Bessie was put out. "I never knew such a child for asking questions. You get on with your painting."

Lucy thought to herself that Personal Remarks must be something rather thrilling to evoke such a telling retort from Bessie, and how lovely to have a blue costume, like the fairy prince's cloak she was trying to paint.

"Why is it," she asked, "that when you want to make someone really beautiful he goes all wrong?"

"How d'you mean?" asked Delia, her deft fingers at work on the crown.

"Well, when I want to make my prince's cloak as glorious

as ever I can, I use all the colours in my box and it looks horrid."

"Of course, 'cos they don't mix. Why don't you give him a blue cloak with a yellow lining?"

"Because," said Lucy truthfully, "I've finished my yellow, and the ultramarine is all mixed up with the Vandyke brown."

Delia sighed. "I suppose you'll have to have my paint-box, but you'll make an awful mess of it. Now just try this crown on first and see if it fits you."

What a tingling mysterious feeling there is in the air to-night! The holly leaves above the cuckoo clock make sharp-cornered shadows on the wall-paper where the Three Jovial Huntsmen for ever wind their horns, and the Pretty Maid tosses her black curls at the inquisitive cavalier. Bessie has reached such an exciting part of her story that her voice has sunk to a whisper. Lucy stirs the paint-stained water in her mug, dreaming of her Poem, and seeing in a coloured cloud the last verses which shall join the tattered threads and bring her wandering characters—the Prince, the Good Fairy, the Magician,the robin and the reindeer—to a happy ending.

Outside in the dark the dogs have started barking, and from somewhere far away in the house there is the sound of voices and opening doors; then down the passage they hear—

"Children, children! Come quick and listen! The carol-singers are here!" and they rush out of the nursery, pell-mell, before Louisa can get at them with brush and comb or mention of clean pinafores—for this is Christmas Eve and the carol-singers have come to sing in the hall.

They came in, scraping their feet and clearing their throats, and stood in a circle under the swinging lamp, facing inwards, their eyes fixed on their leader, Mr. Jenkins the Shoes. Lucy sat on the bend of the stairs from where she could see the wave in Johnny Dowster's hair, the gap in Bill Morgan's front teeth and the way the lump in Mr. Elias Jones's throat worked

up and down when he sang. Mr. Jenkins gave the signal and
they began, very softly at first.

> "See amid the winter's snow,
> Born for us on Earth below;
> See the tender lamb appears
> Promised from eternal years."

Lucy was not sure whether they meant Jesus or the first
forlorn little lamb that would soon be born in the winter
fields. The two grew confused in her mind: she knew only
that it was something young and tender which had braved the
cold and harshness of the world, something which might be
hurt if she did not do something to help it, if she did not wrap
it safely in her arms.

The carol ended; they were consulting together as to what
they should sing next. Lucy wished they would sing for ever
and that she might sit there safe in the shadow, smelling the
pungent scent of the bruised ivy leaves hanging round the
lamp. Now they were singing about the ivy:

> "The holly and the ivy now both are full well grown,
> Of all the trees that spring in wood the holly bears the
> crown;
> The holly bears a blossom as white as lily flower,
> And Mary bore sweet Jesus, to be our sweet Saviour.
>
> The holly bears a berry as red as any blood,
> And Mary bore sweet Jesus, to make poor sinners good;
> The holly bears a prickle as sharp as any thorn,
> And Mary bore sweet Jesus on Christmas day in the
> morn."

It was a sad, dark tune, and now Lucy understood that
nothing she could do would keep the little lamb of God from

being hurt. How cold it had grown suddenly! They had all lost their way in the dark wood, and the sharp leaves of the holly were wet with blood.

"Lucy," her mother called, "why are you hiding up there? Come down and help pass round the mince-pies."

So it was all right, after all. She came slowly down the stairs, shook hands with the carol-singers and handed round the dish of pies. They smelt warm and spicy and she and Delia were told they might each have one for supper. Lucy climbed on her father's knee and rubbed her cheek against the roughness of his tweed coat. She felt deliciously drowsy—the terror of darkness and the cruel, bleeding holly leaves quite forgotten. To-morrow was Christmas Day; to-night they would hang up their stockings.

Chapter Sixteen

Madoc's Moat

ONE day they woke up and there was a white light on the bedroom ceiling and snow outside, and footsteps across the field to show which way Beedles had come that morning. The hills looked nearer than usual and the birds walking on the lawn were puffed out and enormous. After breakfast they took all the tin tea-trays they could find and ran to the Banky Field, but there was not enough snow for tobogganing: blades of green showed through and the trays were very bumpy. Everyone said there would be more snow, and the sky was the colour of pewter behind the white hills. The sheep looked grey and the river was black and very still. On the third snowy night, Madoc's Moat was burnt down.

Madoc's Moat was a house belonging to the children's father on the other side of the valley. It was let to a family named Andrews, who escaped in the middle of the night and ran through the snow in their nightclothes to their nearest neighbours, half-a-mile away. Mr. Andrews was said to have picked up his watch, and Mrs. Andrews a basket of spoons, but everything else was burnt, including, it was to be supposed, all Willie Andrews's toys, since Christmas was only just passed. This thought troubled Lucy very much. She wondered how she would have felt if Henrietta and Anna-Josephine had been burnt. George, Charles and Joseph, she was certain, would have escaped in her arms; never would she have been parted from them.

From pitying Willie Andrews, Lucy came at last to envying him. For a long time she and Delia devised gallant ways in which they would have behaved during the fire: scenes in which they took turns to be the first to notice the smell of burning, to rouse the family from their beds and to run barefoot through the snow carrying Miriam (stupefied with smoke) in their arms.

All through that winter the way to Madoc's Moat was a favourite walk with the children's father, who was full of plans for rebuilding his house, and as often as not he took Delia and Lucy with him. To Lucy it seemed a long walk: the road went up and down over the hills like waves breaking on the shore, and always she hoped that Madoc's Moat would be on top of the next crest; but it wasn't, not for a long time, and sometimes her legs ached before it came in sight.

First, they had to pass the farm of Hissing Geese, and then there was a cottage from which a light-eyed collie rushed out barking. Only when these dangers had been passed did they come at last to Madoc's Moat under the dark wood, with the roof gone and empty, blackened windows gazing across the valley. They would push open the little wicket and go up through the orchard and over what had once been the Andrews's rubbish heap, and then they were there. Sometimes, Mr. Price, the agent, or William Lewis, the builder, would meet them to talk to the children's father, and this was an advantage because it gave Delia and Lucy time for their games, and Madoc's Moat proved one of the best playing-grounds they had ever known.

When there was time to spare, Delia went indoors (if you could call "indoors" a house with no roof) and Lucy ran down to the drive gate and stepped into an imaginary brougham, as though she were paying calls in her prettiest clothes, with a card-case in her hand. Then she turned into a horse and pranced up the drive between the laurels and rhododendrons, drawing up on the gravel sweep before the front door. Alighting with dignity from her carriage she mounted the stone steps and pulled the bell-handle; but the bell did not ring, for the wire had been burnt and the bell had fallen off and was lost. As soon as she had stuffed the bellhandle back in its hole, Delia appeared on the threshold with her lips pursed together like Sarah's when she answered the front door and showed people into the drawing-room.

"Is Mrs. Fitzgerald in," asked Lucy, in a high, peculiar voice.

"Yes, ma'am. Please to step this way, ma'am," replied Delia, and led the way into the only room which still possessed a floor. Not only had it a floor, but there were strips of blue paper hanging on the walls and a grate where, on white and yellow tiles, were pictures of men reaping and women carrying sheaves of corn. These tiles were slightly blackened by smoke; not by the appalling smoke and flame which had driven the Andrews family into the snowy night, but by everyday, cheerful fires round which they had sat talking with their feet on the fender. Now there was nothing at all left in that room, except the springs of chairs lying like coiled serpents on the floor. The window-frame, with its view of brown fields and winding river, was black charcoal which came off on your fingers when you rubbed it.

It was queer, thought Lucy, that, however good a game they had, no part of it was half so pleasant as the moment of driving up, full of expectation, to the front door. Left alone in the drawing-room, while Delia went to inform Mrs. Fitzgerald of her presence, she grew a little frightened. Suppose Delia did not come back? Suppose she fell into the cellar, over the threshold of the dining-room, where already the grass was beginning to grow among the broken wine-bottles? Suppose her father forgot them both (ridiculous thought) and went home, or away into the dark wood that came creeping down behind the house? Then just as she could bear it no longer, Delia would hurry in with outstretched hands saying: "My dear, how good of you to call! Tell me, how are you keeping"

"I'm keeping quite well, thank you," said Lucy, and added under her breath, "Oh, Delia, doesn't it sound like apples!"

Delia looked annoyed. "Grown-ups often say that. How is

your husband?" she added in bright, conversational tones.

"Well," said Lucy, "he has a great many tiresome meetings. I'm afraid he'll wear himself out."

"Tut! tut!" said Delia.

Lucy wished she had thought of that herself; it was so conclusive.

"My children are giving me a lot of trouble," Delia continued, in a care-worn voice. "I can't get them to attend to their lessons. I really think I shall have to hire a governess."

"Mine are no trouble at all," Lucy interposed. "George and Charles spend their whole time studying volumes."

"Volumes of what," asked Delia.

"Oh, just volumes," said Lucy. "Volumes mean something difficult, don't they, But Joseph," she went on, and her voice softened on the word, for Joseph was her darling, "Joseph plays the violin all day. Would you like to hear him play now?" she asked hastily. "He's just outside with the horses."

"Very well," said Mrs. Fitzgerald, "if his shoes aren't too muddy. Boys never wipe their feet properly. I'll be getting the tea ready," she added.

Lucy ran out to call Joseph, and Delia fetched some pieces of broken crockery from what had once been the pantry. She was setting them out on the floor when Lucy returned, doubling the role of Joseph and his proud mother.

Joseph did not need much persuasion; his fiddle and bow were ever ready, and, while Mrs. Fitzgerald arranged her tea-party, the gifted young musician leaned in the corner of the room and drew his invisible bow over an invisible instrument.

To anyone else it might have seemed that Lucy was humming in a peculiar way with her top teeth over her lower lip, while the fingers of her left hand lovingly caressed the air, and her right arm moved to and fro with great rapidity; but Mrs. Fitzgerald realised that she was in the presence of a master.

"That's very nice. Now will you play your other tune?" she

said, as Joseph slowed to an end. He had two tunes in his repertoire—one was Mignon's song, "Kennst du das Land?", and the other an air from Rigoletto, with many flourishes. They were lifelike imitations of the two sides of a gramophone record which Lucy admired.

"The tea's getting a little stewed," Mrs. Fitzgerald continued. "Perhaps you'd better come now."

Joseph sighed and wiped his mouth. "It's not so good as usual to-day," he said. "I can't get the high notes without spitting, but the pizzi what-you-call-it was awfully good, don't you think?"

"Not bad," said Mrs. Fitzgerald. "Try some of this home-made cake. Would Joseph like some too?"

"I think not. He'd probably prefer having tea in the saddle-room with the coachman, if you don't mind. You know," Lucy went on, "Joseph is really a very odd boy. The kind of things that other people like very much he likes just a little bit, and the things that other people find ordinary he likes extremely."

"What kind of things?"

"Oh, things like holes in trees, and stirring pigs' food, and watching grown-ups dress and undress, and being in the potting-shed when Jarman fries his bacon for dinner, and slapping butter about when they're churning, and riding in the spring-cart ever so much better than in the other carriages."

"But that's you," Delia objected. "Not Joseph."

"We're rather alike," said Lucy, "but not really the same. I enjoy other things too, but Joseph only likes the queer ones. And when we go for walks and other people say 'What a beautiful view!' Joseph isn't thinking that at all. He likes the muddy lanes that go twisting in and out, and the little trees blown crooked in the wind, and water where it lies on top of a weir and curves over the edge, gently, gently, before it goes crashing down below. I like new clothes, but Joseph prefers old ones, and he can't bear throwing away anything, in case it feels sad; even things like shoes and toothbrushes."

"I've seen you muttering things to your old toothbrushes," said Delia.

Lucy flushed. "That was probably Joseph, not me."

"Well, I think it's silly," said Delia firmly. "You're always saying that Joseph is a separate person and quite real, and now you're muddling him up with yourself."

"But he is real," Lucy insisted. "He's the most real person that ever was. He's more real than I am."

"Oh, very well," said Delia. "There's Daddy calling us. Help me clear away the tea-things."

Before they set out for home, they called at Martha Hamer's cottage in the dingle. Martha had once been a kitchen-maid at Pengarth before she married Hamer, who was weak and weedy and came sometimes to help in the cider-making or the pig-killing. Martha's cottage was at the bottom of the dingle. The wet purplish-brown leaves of the oak trees were drifted round the door, and the noise of the stream was so loud that you had to shout to make yourself heard. Martha seemed very pleased to see them and they stood crowded inside the cottage, which smelt hot and damp, like the ironing room at Pengarth. Martha was hot and damp too and very wide, instead of going in in one place and out in another, like most ladies. Her children came out shyly from behind pieces of furniture. There were a great number of them.

"How many now, Martha," asked Mr. Gwyn. "Six, is it?"

Martha said "No, it was seven," and she bent down and pulled a box out from under the table, and in it was a tiny, dark red baby. Mr. Gwyn laughed and said it was as good as a conjuring trick, and Delia asked if she might hold it in her arms. So she sat on the settle and Martha gave her the baby. After that Lucy wanted to hold it too. The baby smelt of flannel and waved its fists about in the air. Delia put one of her fingers inside its fist, and the baby held on tight. Its name was Edward Cadwalader.

Mr. Gwyn asked Martha if she had had a good Christmas,

and she said "Middling"; and he asked how Hamer was getting on, and she said, "Indeed, very middling; his cough was something awful at night, but the children were right sharp."

Then Mr. Gwyn gave each of the children some money from his pocket and said Mrs. Gwyn would be coming over soon to see the baby, and Delia put Edward Cadwalader back very carefully in his box, and they came away. All the six children stood watching them from the door as they climbed out of the dingle, away from the wet leaves and the rushing stream.

They set out on the way home, with the fiery sunset before them. Above the familiar line of the hills great copper clouds were piled, fantastic mountain shapes guarding a remote, golden sea. When they passed the farm of Hissing Geese a boy was driving the cows home from a field across the road.

"The lowing herd wind slowly o'er the lea," said the children's father, and Lucy asked what was a "lowing herd." He explained, and then said, "Have you never heard that before? It's a grand poem."

Lucy said, "Please say it," and he did, and it was grand and the way home seemed shorter than usual. There was one bit which, although she did not understand it, sent shivers of pleasure down Lucy's back.

> "For who, to dumb Forgetfulness a prey,
> This pleasing anxious being e'er resigned,
> Left the warm precincts of the cheerful day
> Nor cast one longing, lingering look behind?"

The "cheerful day" was fading in the sky before them, and Lucy looked behind over her shoulder at the glimmering walls of Madoc's Moat, with its burnt-out windows, and the dark dingle below where Martha's new baby was lying. Her father had stopped reciting to whistle to the dogs; then he went on, and it was the same lovely stuff:

> "E'en from the tomb the voice of Nature cries,
> E'en in our Ashes live their wonted Fires."

The "wonted fires," Lucy thought, were there, round the setting sun, reflected in the wet road and the western windows of the cottages. But the lines filled her with unexplained sadness. The word "tomb" was so cold. "If they put Joseph in a tomb," she thought, "I should hear him cry. That must be the voice of Nature."

The light was dying behind the hill as they climbed over the railway bridge and dropped into the home lane, and the owls hooted in the trees beside the river. Delia and Lucy fastened the reluctant dogs into their kennel and ran indoors. A delicious smell of fresh, warm bread came from the kitchen. They could still hear the owls hooting outside as they climbed the back stairs and took off their muddy boots under the glimmering square of window.

"Joseph is very fond of poetry," said Lucy, slowly unlacing her boots. "He's written some himself. Would you like to hear it?"

"No," said Delia. "I'm much too hungry. Hurry up with your boots."

She buttoned her slippers and ran down the passage. Lucy sat, pulling the laces through her fingers; one of them had a broken tag which caught every time in the hole. She tried to remember the poetry her father had recited, but found she had forgotten it all, except "wonted fires," and a "lingering look behind." What "lingering" things boots were! There was no end of them; after you'd taken them off in the evening you had to put them on again in the morning, and be scolded for keeping everyone waiting. She searched for her slippers on the dark lower shelf and stood up for a last glance through the window. There was no light anywhere now except on the river, which gleamed between its banks, and in the sky, where a solitary star shone over the hill.

"Joseph and I will write lots and lots of poetry," thought Lucy to herself.

The owl hooted once more.

She went down the passage and opened the nursery door. The room was so bright with lamplight and firelight that at first she stood blinking on the threshold. The tea-table was laid and Louisa was tying Miriam's bib under her chin. Maurice was lying face downwards on the floor, trying excitedly to tell Delia something. When he saw Lucy he started all over again.

"I've got a new game. I write letters to Mrs. Bannister and I drop them through the crack in the floor and they fall down into the kitchen and Mrs. Bannister calls out the answers. She's been baking and I wrote a letter and asked her to make me a little tiny loaf, and she did, and I'm going to eat it for tea."

"We saw Martha's new baby," said Delia. "It's called Edward Cadwalader and she let me hold it."

"And me," said Lucy.

"Stop chattering, all of you, and draw up your chairs properly and quietly to the tea-table," said Louisa.

Chapter Seventeen

Firelight

Before January had ended all the children caught colds. The two little ones sniffed and snuffled all day in the nursery under Louisa's eye, but Delia and Lucy were really bad and lay in bed, their chests well rubbed with camphorated oil and a fire blazing up the chimney. Lucy wrote a poem with which she was pleased, although the first lines were rather a crib from William Blake:

> Fire, fire, burning bright
> In my bedroom all the night,
> How I love to see you blaze
> And at you for long I gaze,
> Till at last my eyelids drop
> And I slumber like a top.

But afterwards, when her cold grew worse and she wheezed like the harmonium in Pengarth Church and could not sleep without dark, fantastic dreams, she altered the middle lines to:

> How I hate to see you burn
> As in my bed I twist and turn.

Delia soon recovered and was allowed to walk about the house, wearing a shawl in the passages. She employed her time painting all the illustrations in "The Crimson Fairy Book," and labelling the flowers she had pressed the summer before. They looked brown and dejected, poor things; although Delia wrote under each one such names as

"Stitchwort," "Lady's Smock" and "Coltsfoot" in her best "Jackson's Upright Copy Book" handwriting, it was difficult to imagine that these flattened corpses had once blown in the fields or nestled happily under green hedges.

But Lucy stayed in bed with a head that ached too much to invent any more poetry, or even to read books to herself. She spent a great deal of time drawing imaginary pictures on the ceiling with one finger— pictures of knights on horseback, and ladies with flying hair, running, running as fast as they could through haunted woods. These pictures naturally vanished as soon as they were made, and the grownups discouraged the practice. They said that Lucy looked like a half-wit, lying in bed, waggling her finger at the ceiling; but the moment they were out of the room she began again, though it was hard to explain to anyone the fascination of that blank, white ceiling —like an enormous drawing-book with no need of an india-rubber.

When she was tired of drawing there was always the screen with which to pass the time. This screen had been made a great many years before by Shân and her friends when they were young, and now it had been carried into the bedroom to keep the draught from Lucy's head. It did far more than keep away draughts; it provided a world in which a sick child's fancy might wander all day and not grow weary.

Under a coating of golden-brown varnish the strangest things occurred, without trouble or inconvenience, since paste and scissors had made all things equal. Time, space, geography and proportion were obliterated and the most incompatible happenings were matched, sobered and pickled for ever in the amber of varnish and slow time. Here a stage-coach lumbered along a road which ended in a waterfall, and under the waterfall ladies and gentlemen in straw boaters and "bustles" played a serene game of croquet. Here Christian was armed for his meeting with Apollyon by the sisters Discretion, Prudence, Piety and Charity; while near by, two

children and a collie-dog crossed a daisied meadow on their
way to school. Crumbling ruins, outlined against a moonlit
sky, got strangely mixed with a flock of gigantic geese; a
gentleman with side whiskers, romantically climbing a ladder,
was obviously about to step into a room where a bishop in
gaiters slept in a chair, and a lady, twice as big as the ladder,
played and sang plaintively at the piano.

Lucy was roused from dreaming contemplation of these
scenes to find Shân sitting in the bedroom chair of creaking
cane, with her feet on the fender and her skirt turned up over
her knees. She had thrown on another log, and the firelight
leapt and sparkled on the buckles of her kid slippers and the
shot purple silk of her petticoat.

"Darling, how are you feeling?" asked Shân. "Shall I read
you 'Little Lord Fauntleroy'? It's such a nice book."

"No, thank you," said Lucy. "I'd rather you talked instead.
Tell me about your old and ancient, lineaged times."

She did not say this because she did not like Shân's
reading, though indeed she had a way of dozing in the middle
of a sentence, so that they bribed her by placing a piece of
toffee on the mantelpiece, promising she might have it if she
kept awake; a manoeuvre which Shân outwitted by declaring
she would wake up if they gave her the toffee and then
dropping asleep with it in her mouth. But Lucy had a feeling
that David would despise the adventures of the curled and
velvet-clad Cedric and his "dearest" Mama. The book he
would expect her to read was "The Young Fur Traders," or
"The Treasure of the Incas," and her head ached far too much
to-day to want either of them. So she asked instead for "old
and ancient, lineaged times"—as she called them—and settled
down with a sigh of contentment to listen.

Of course they began in the usual way, Shân declaring she
could not remember a thing and Lucy prompting.

"Tell me about the time you slid down a ladder in your new
blue frock."

Or again: "Tell me how you pretended a wardrobe was a sea-cliff, and how you took off all your clothes, and dived on to the floor, and grandfather came in and found you."

But to-day Shân was bored with those old tales; the sight of the screen reminded her of the days when she was eighteen. Perhaps there really was a magic quality about that screen.

In her soft voice, that was like the touch of her plump, ringed fingers, Shân described the dress in which she had gone to her first ball—a pink silk dress with rosebuds round the waist, and bunches of rosebuds here and there on her skirt. There was a little pair of pink silk slippers too, but, if you had to drive a long way to the ball in a brougham over snowy roads, then it was well to wear a pair of bedroom shoes, knitted in ugly brown wool, but comforting to the ankles on a cold night. And if you drove up to the dark house and saw the lighted windows and the fiddlers' elbows moving, and heard the music, playing so sweetly and headily, so that you were in terror lest you should have missed one moment of it, then it was natural that you should fling off your shawls and capes and run into the ballroom, dancing with your head in a whirl and your heart as light as thistle-down. Only in the middle of the dance, under the lighted candles, would you make the awful discovery and behold your tripping, foolish feet encased in brown woollen shoes. That is what happened to Shân at her first ball.

Then there were the Visits she paid to her friend Emily, and Emily's brother Tom, who would come to meet her at the station with a high-spirited chestnut horse. One Christmas time Shan wore a new scarlet cape, edged with fur. Every day they skated on a frozen lake among the hills, and came back to find roaring fires in their bedrooms and their prettiest frocks laid out ready to put on. There was a strawcoloured one, said Shân, with knots of blue ribbon on the shoulders which suited her well; and every evening she and Tom played and sang together at the piano. In the spring she went abroad with Tom and Emily and their parents. They drove in a diligence over the Alps into Italy and were dug out of a snow-drift at the top of the pass. Afterwards they stayed on the shores of a lake, and Tom would row them in a boat while he and Shân still sang duets. The sun shone all day and they would land on a little island, half smothered in wistaria.

While Shân was talking the fire crackled in the chimney and a buzzing fly blundered against the ceiling, a foolish lost fly who must have been deluded by the warm room into thinking it was summer-time. But Lucy liked to hear him. She closed her eyes and immediately she saw herself in the morning-room downstairs, the window wide open and the room full of light and the scent of wallflowers. She saw herself lying on the floor in a pool of sunshine, chalking the pictures in "The Pilgrim's Progress." Then she opened her eyes quickly, and there were the bare dripping trees standing outside the window in the January dusk, and Shân nodding by the fire.

In the same way, Shân had only to close her eyes in order to see herself in a pink dress covered with rosebuds, dancing in a pair of bedroom slippers; or seated in a boat in the middle of a blue, Italian lake. One thing was "real," the other only "make-up," yet it seemed to Lucy that the "make-up" was often the more important of the two, though of course you could not say this to grown-ups, who nearly all lived in an entirely "real" world. Yet how easily one stepped out of it! When Maurice, who had a secret fondness for dolls, said "Pretend I'm not a boy!" he was immediately free to play at tea-parties to his heart's content.

In the same way, whenever Lucy did a puppet play for Maurice and Miriam's entertainment on the nursery table, with pieces of holly for a forest and the round mirror for a lake, the play she was so busy inventing, producing and acting all at the same moment—was far more "real" to her than the ordinary dull nursery, with Louisa sitting in the rocking-chair, mending stockings.

How did grown-ups manage to exist all day with so little invention? They even dressed in the morning without imagining themselves other than they were, whereas Lucy felt that she could never bear to put on her clothes at all if she were not consoled at every phase by pretending to be someone else—the Young Acrobat, the White Lady or the Innocent Child.

It would, she thought with some vanity, be dull for the others if she were not there to amuse them; but, on the other hand, where would she be without an audience? She could no more produce a puppet play without first cajoling the two youngest into listening than the dogs could take themselves for walks without human companionship.

Delia might linger a little over unlacing her boots on the back landing while Lucy turned it into the besieged castle of Lady Isabelle, but, after all, she could unlace them without this accompaniment; whereas it was impossible to produce Lady Isabelle unless Delia were there to listen. It was not, of course, Delia's presence that turned the door into Lord Edward and the door-knob into his mailed fist, and yet, so long as she remained a willing, or even an impatient audience, Lucy knew that they were both in a castle keep and in peril of their lives. No sooner had Delia taken herself off than castle and lady crumbled, and Lucy herself became a little girl who was late for lunch. The rest of her world, it seemed, could live without "makeup," but Lucy—to whom invention mattered so much —could not get on at all without real people. It was rather humiliating.

The coals fell apart in the grate and a flame leapt up the chimney. It threw a familiar shadow on the ceiling—the shadow, it seemed to Lucy, of a clergyman in a surplice who ran up a long flight of steps and bobbed up and down in the pulpit.

"Hallo," she said to him. "You do think a lot of yourself, don't you? But it's no use trying to frighten me. I know exactly what you are: you're nothing but the shadow of the bed-post."

But the clergyman only nodded, growing sometimes tall and then shrinking till there was nothing left of him but a squat, leering head.

"Don't do that," said Lucy. "It's rude, and after all I invented you. You ought to be glad you're alive."

But the clergyman paid no attention.

"I was only an invention, but I've got the better of you now," he seemed to say.

"Shân, Shân, wake up," said Lucy loudly.

"What's that, darling? I wasn't asleep, you know. Now what were we talking about? Some nonsense about Emily and the old days. How dark it's grown! It's high time you had your medicine."

She lit the two candles on the dressing-table, and immediately there were new shadows everywhere and the nodding clergyman faded into unimportance.

"Shân," said Lucy, "were you ever frightened of the things you invented yourself?"

"I don't remember." Shân was searching for the bottle and spoon. "Emily was a great one for inventing things—such droll rhymes and riddles. We used to write them in each other's albums."

"Those must have been nice inventions. Some of mine are dreadful."

"Then stop thinking about them," said Shân briskly, "and drink your medicine."

Chapter Eighteen

Tramp and Treacle

The Rev. Daniel Vaughan had been ill all winter, and when April came, he and his wife went away for a month or more. His place every Sunday was taken by Mr. Price from the neighbouring church of Llandre. The river divided the parishes, nor was there any bridge immediately between the two churches facing each other on opposite sides of the valley, so that the Rector of Llandre had to walk in a half-circle of some three miles before he could reach Pengarth. As the weather grew warmer this walk became irksome, and Mr. Price took to wading across the river, choosing carefully that part where it flowed wide and shallow and prattled gently over the stones.

He was a dreamy, unpunctual bachelor and seldom arrived on time. At eleven o'clock the congregation of Pengarth would assemble in the churchyard, scanning the valley until at last they perceived the little figure of Mr. Price hurrying across the fields and sitting down on the far side of the river to remove his shoes and stockings and roll up his trousers.

"Jowks! The watter's ris in the night. Stick to it, man!" exclaimed Davey Pugh, spitting over the graveyard wall.

"Oh, nem-o-dearl There's drowned he'll be!" piped old Ann Elias. But the sturdy figure of the Rector of Llandre pushed on through the swirling stream, and a murmur of relief went up as he was seen to climb the willowed bank and, sitting down on the grass, wipe his feet with a pocket-handkerchief; at which point Abel, the Rector's garden-boy, ran into the church and gave Martin, the verger, the signal to start ringing the five-minute bell. When the service was over, Mr. Price would hurry back the way he had come, since he had a Sunday School service to conduct at Llandre in the afternoon. Often he left his second pair of spectacles behind in the vestry, and then either Abel or the swift-footed Jarman would pursue him across fields and flood.

The Vaughan children had been left behind at the Rectory in the care of their Aunt Hetty. One day towards the end of April, she wrote a note to Mrs. Gwyn and sent it to Pengarth by Fitton, a rosy-cheeked old man with an impediment in his speech who had once tried a barber's trade and now lived by carrying the Rectory washing and doing errands in town for the Pengarth cottagers. As soon as Lucy, who was sailing boats with Maurice on the stable tank, heard Fitton stuttering at the back-door, she guessed that there was a message from the Rectory and ran round to the front of the house. A few minutes later, her mother called to her from a window; Miss Vaughan had written to say that next day was David's birthday, and to ask if Lucy would spend it at the Rectory.

"You must take David a present," said Lucy's mother. "I think I have a box of soldiers in my cupboard. And you will both try to be good, won't you, and not give poor Miss Hetty any trouble?"

Lucy promised and went to bed that evening full of plans and dreams.

Next morning, Beedles drove her up to the Rectory. He took the spring-cart as he was on his way to buy a new litter of pigs at the fair. Beedles clicked his tongue against his teeth, Beauty shook herself and stepped out into a brisk trot, and the spring-cart swung rapturously from side to side over the road between the white hawthorn bushes and the wet green fields, where the larks poured themselves out in song. David was standing in the road outside the Rectory when they turned the corner.

"I heard you coming half a mile away," he remarked. "What's inside that parcel?"

Lucy jumped down on to the road. "It's for you, to wish

you many happy returns; and oh, what do you think! Beedles is going to buy six baby pigs and he says I can christen them all; but I'll let you name one if you want to very much."

"I know what this is," said David. "It's soldiers. I can hear them rattling. Come on, and I'll show you a new fortress I've constructed behind the rubbish heap."

"Good-bye, Beedles. Promise faithfully not to christen the pigs till I see them," cried Lucy and ran after David.

The fortress was made of mown grass from the Rectory lawn, after it had been tipped out of a barrow behind the stable. The new lead soldiers, in their shiny red jackets, looked very fine on the green mounds and valleys which David and Lucy dug with their fingers in the cool, damp grass, for the lawn had been recently mown for the first time that year. Then David said, "I've thought of an even better place—just like real fortifications. Martin's digging old Mrs. Powell's grave. Let's take them there."

They went out through the little wicket from the garden into the graveyard, past the bushes of flowering currant, which smelt very sweet. Martin had been digging the grave since early morning and now he had knocked off to eat his bait and drink a cup of tea in the Rectory kitchen. Two planks of wood edged the open grave and a mound of bright brown soil was heaped up beside it. There the children set about their battle. They divided the soldiers between them and arranged them in single formation among the rugged lumps of earth.

"It's like a mountain in Asia," said David. "Shall we pretend it's the Indian Mutiny, or Akbar?"

"Akbar," replied Lucy. "He's much more exciting."

"But Akbar's troops had turbans and scimitars," David objected.

"Well, isn't it quite easy to imagine turbans and scimitars?" said Lucy.

"Let's make a tunnel through the earth. I'll start my end,

and you start yours, and we'll meet in the middle," David suggested.

"Do you think we ought to?" said Lucy with sudden misgiving.

"Who's to mind? Martin's talking to Mary Ellen."

David flung himself down on the ground and started to burrow like a terrier. Lucy followed suit, but the earth got into her finger-nails and she did not like it.

"No, I won't, David," she said firmly. "I shall build a palace for Akbar instead," and she started to gather loose stones and lined them with moss and primroses from under the hedge. The warm sun shone down from the sky and a cuckoo called again and again from the hill; the valley below the graveyard was full of the high cries of lambs and the deep answering notes of sheep; the lambs were white as the hawthorn trees. When Lucy half-closed her eyes the brightness of the spring sunshine broke into a thousand shafts of splintered light; she felt sleepy and at the same time wide awake. Looking down into the half-dug grave she wondered how it would feel to be shut up in the dark; if one were sleepy—really sleepy—perhaps one wouldn't mind very much.

Presently the gate of the churchyard opened and a tramp slouched inside.

"Hullo," said David, sitting up. "What do you want?"

The tramp was a tall man, but his shoulders drooped so that he looked old and bent. He had a red handkerchief round his neck and the back of his coat hung in tatters. His boots were white with dust and tied with string.

"I could do with something to eat," grumbled the tramp in a voice which was quite different from the voices of the people who lived in Pengarth. "And a pair of your father's boots, young sir, if he has them to spare."

"My father's not at home and I can't give away his boots,"

said David, "and if I were you, I shouldn't go to the house. Mary Ellen's busy and Aunt Hetty's scared of tramps."

"Oh, it's tramps, is it?" shouted the man. "What right 'ave you got to call me names, I'd like ter know, if an honest man can't get work? Why don't you blame the rotten country? 'Aven't I walked all the way from Cardiff? And the bloody Unions taking it out of a chap till you might as well be dead, I tell you, dead and rotted and shovelled away in there." He nodded at the grave. "That's a queer place for two kids to be playing in, anyway. Wotcher getting at?"

"We're playing soldiers, really," said Lucy, "but now I've begun to build a royal palace. Won't you sit down if you're so tired?"

"Well, I don't mind if I does," said the man more quietly, and he sat down on the green mound of a grave that was so old that no one knew any longer to whom it belonged.

"Oh, your poor boots!" said Lucy. "They're all broken. I'm so sorry. Why don't you take them off? Louisa always feels better when she does; she says it rests her corns."

Lucy wasn't sure what corns were exactly, but the tramp looked as though he might have them, and besides they sounded grown-up. The man gave her a strange glance and began to unlace his boots. His grimy toes stuck up through the holes in his socks, but he stretched them out on the soft warm grass and took a clay pipe out of his pocket and for a time they were all silent.

"Who they going to put in there?" he asked presently, jerking his pipe in the direction of the grave.

"Old Mrs. Powell," said David. "She was a bit queer and lived all alone on the hill."

"She'll be alone all right in there," said the man.

"Oh, no, she won't," said David quickly. "Only her body will be there; the real Mrs. Powell won't be there at all, and perhaps she won't be queer any longer. My father says we shall all be different."

Lucy interrupted him. "Look, quickl Both of youl The loveliest butterfly!"

"Shall I catch it?" asked David. "You could hold it while I run and fetch my killing-bottle."

"No, don't," said Lucy. "Please don't. I've just thought of something." She sat up excitedly. "Supposing it isn't a butterfly at all. Suppose it's really Mrs. Powelll"

They all three sat in silence watching the butterfly hover over the open grave. The tramp was the first to speak.

"Go on!" he said. "Wot's the use of talking? We're 'ere, aren't we? We're not flitting about in the air. I ain't 'ad no breakfast and I don't see myself gettin' no dinner neither."

"I'll tell you what I'll do," said Lucy, jumping up. "I'll go and ask Mary Ellen for something and pretend it's for David and me."

She ran to the house, and found Mary Ellen in the kitchen.

"Oh, Mary Ellen, we're so hungry. Will you give us some bread-and-butter7"

"Well now, Miss Lucy, it's past twelve and there's a leg of mutton for lunch and a good treacle pudding. You'll spoil your appetite if you go eating between meals."

"Only a bite, Mary Ellen. Just for a treat, 'cos it's David's birthday."

"Well, well," said Mary Ellen, drying her hands. "You're a pair of you for getting round folks." She cut two generous slices of bread, spread them thickly with treacle and gave them to Lucy. "Master David loves treacle, I know," she said, and added, "There's a nasty-looking tramp hanging round. One of them stole all our eggs last week. Tell Master David to keep a look-out."

"I'll tell him," said Lucy and sped away.

The tramp had put on his boots and was standing with hunched shoulders in the churchyard path.

"Mary Ellen's put treacle on them," said Lucy, thrusting

both slices into his hands. "I pretended I wanted it as a birthday treat for David."

The man took the bread without a word. At the gate he turned and said, "Good luck, Missy."

"Good-bye, good-bye," called the children, but he did not turn his head again, only shuffled on down the sunny road between the young green of the hedges.

"He might have said 'Good luck' to you. After all, it's your birthday," said Lucy indignantly.

"And it was my treacle," said David. "I hate tramps; they smell horrid."

"Poor, poor man," said Lucy softly. "Here's Martin coming to dig. Let's go and play somewhere else."

Chapter Nineteen

The Beginning of the End

At the beginning of the summer David and Delia went away to school. Now, for the first time, the long, timeless days of the year were trapped and divided into terms and holidays, and David, after a day spent in the company of boy cousins, was heard to refer, quite casually, to "next hols."

Until now their lives had been governed by the seasons. The year began with snow on the hills and patches of snowdrops in the grass; the first hedgesparrow's eggs and the wild, sweet cry of the curlew meant spring; drifting blossom and the white spray of cow-parsley brought summer— exquisite, endless summer when a fine day was good enough excuse for banishing lesson books and packing a picnic basket. By the time autumn came round once more Lucy had almost forgotten what winter was like and Miriam could not remember anything at all about it. The day on which Jarman finished picking the apples was the signal for trying on their last winter's clothes: scratchy garments, grown short in the sleeve and smelling of moth balls. Delia's were passed on to Lucy, and Lucy's were put away to wait for Miriam.

This summer Lucy inherited a great many of Delia's clothes, and Delia became the owner of a dazzling new outfit. It included such strange things as a gym. tunic, a liberty bodice and a glossy tennis racquet— for hitherto they had shared impartially such racquets as were discarded by their aunts and parents. There were also a shiny black trunk, a dressing-gown of pale blue and a Sunday hat, with a pink velvet bow in front, which Lucy thought the most beautiful object she had ever seen. Delia went about in big-eyed solemnity, while Louisa sat for days sewing names on to stockings and underclothes. A sense of doom hung heavy in the spring sunshine.

David's term started first, and on the day before he left home all the Rectory children came to tea. They had planned to spend their time birds'-nesting, but all afternoon the rain fell heavily and Louisa said they must stay indoors.

Delia took Peggy and Olwen up to her bedroom to admire her new clothes and (Lucy suspected) to play with her dolls, for of late Delia had grown shy of being seen in public with Anna-Josephine and dear Henrietta.

In the nursery David and Lucy knelt in front of the low window-seat, making plasticine models. Outside the rain fell softly in the garden and the thrushes in the lilac bushes were singing their hearts out for pleasure at the soft spring day. David was making a boat and a pair of oars out of the best blue plasticine, while Lucy, with a messy piece of uncertain colour, was engaged on the delicate and difficult task of fashioning a teapot.

"I've got an idea," said David suddenly. "When I come home I'll ask your father to let us have your old canoe—the one the horse stepped in—and we'll mend it and play Red Indians. I'll be Hawk-Eye, and you can be Chingachgook if you like," he added magnanimously.

"Daddy says we mayn't go in the canoe till we can swim across the river, and I can swim only ten strokes and then I get all puffed," Lucy objected.

"There's a swimming-bath at school," said David. "When I come back I'll teach you."

"And when you come back for always will you marry me, and then we can go away on a voyage together?" asked Lucy rapidly, struggling with the teapot spout.

"I'm not sure," he said thoughtfully. "You see, I'm going round the world first and that's no place for women."

"Oh, but, David, do let me come too! Think of Cora and Alice in 'The Last of the Mohicans.' They went everywhere."

"Cora and Alice were sloppy," said David. "But you wouldn't be that. I daresay I'll take you. Anyway, I promise I won't take anyone else. You can have this boat as a keepsake if you like," he added, after a moment's pause.

"And I'll give you this teapot, though it's not nearly as beautiful as your boat."

"Oh, that's all right," he said amiably. "I've seen worse."

They did not tell anyone about the keepsakes, and Lucy hid hers in the dolls' medicine chest—a tin box where she kept an empty thermometer-case, and a bottle of gargle mixture that had once belonged to Miss Crabtree. But at tea, when Olwen was being particularly annoying and mysterious over their games upstairs, Lucy burst out with:

"I know what you were doing. You were just playing with the dolls. But David and I were making plans—really exciting plans; you'll never know anything about them—and when we grow up we're going to be married."

"Whose idea was that," asked Olwen sceptically.

"Well, I suggested it," said Lucy, with truth.

"You would!" remarked Louisa as she filled up the teapot.

Next day they went down to the Banky Field, which runs close by the railway, to see David's train go by. Louisa kindly allowed them to take a towel from the night nursery with which to wave, and she came herself with Miriam, "to see the last of Master David," as she put it, for she was fond of him and never scolded much, even when he forgot to wash his hands before coming to tea, and led Lucy into places where she tore her clothes.

The Banky Field was bright with buttercups and their shoes were powdered gold by the time they reached the hump that overlooks the railway. A cuckoo called loudly from the curly young leaves of an oak tree by the gate and then flew clumsily across the silver loop of the river. There was a cloud of bluebells in the corner of the bottom hay-field, and beyond the river they could see Mrs. Bound's geese and six yellow goslings. The children sat down to wait and Delia began to make a daisy-chain for Miriam.

One of the earliest things that Lucy could remember was being brought down to this field to see King Edward go by. After the train had passed everyone argued as to which was the King. Lucy alone insisted that she had seen him, and was mortified when one of the grown-ups discovered that it was the engine-driver to whom she had waved her flag, since she had imagined that anyone so glorious as a king would be sure to travel in that proud position.

But that was years ago, when she was no bigger than Miriam, rolling among the buttercups. Now she felt old, so old, and in three days Delia would have gone and she would be the eldest of the family. "You must try to be wise and sensible now," her mother had said, and the words lay heavy on her heart.

Suddenly Maurice shouted: "Here she comes!" There was a puff of smoke and the train came chugging between the green fields. Delia and Lucy each grasped a corner of the towel, and Louisa held Miriam high in her arms. The train drew nearer. Where was David? It rocked and roared over the bridge and there sure enough was David, his face very white under a bowler hat. He waved his handkerchief and went on waving it until there was nothing to be seen but the back of the guard's van. Then they went home soberly. Maurice even forbore to roll all the way down the Banky Field. Only Miriam was delighted with her daisy-chain.

"Well, anyway," said Louisa, "it's something to see Master David with a clean pocket-handkerchief."

Lovely, lovely days of early summer! You were never more lovely at Pengarth than when Delia went away for the first time. The beds, that Jarman had stocked with tawny wallflowers, sent warm breaths into the rooms and the drunken bees rocked through the open windows and out again; the pink may tree at the end of the lawn was hung with coral, and the birds never ceased singing. Indoors the maids had finished the spring cleaning and the house smelt delicately of beeswax.

Even the dolls' house was turned out and the little muslin curtains, freshly starched and ironed, were waiting to be hung at each window. But Delia was too busy trying on her new clothes and having her old ones altered and "let down" by Sally—Davey John's daughter—who was learning to be a dressmaker, but always made everything a little crooked.

So Lucy started all alone to put the furniture back in the dolls' house, but without Delia everything fell into hopeless confusion: some of the kitchen knives and forks had got wedged between the bars of the drawing-room bird-cage; the piano-stool, which had propped up Emily for so many years, was broken in two, and all the bed-clothes were missing. After struggling for half a morning Lucy abandoned the task, although the thought of the poor dolls, prostrate as the victims of an earthquake, troubled her not a little.

Delia had a great many last instructions to impart. There were the dogs, the cats, the guinea-pigs and the tortoise who lived in the greenhouse to feed every day. Delia had never taken her responsibilities lightly: each animal had its appointed meal-time; some of them their own particular plates. Of course, thought Lucy, no one would mind looking after the dogs, since they were nearly as good as other people when it came to company, but about the cats and the guinea-pigs she was not so sure. The guinea-pigs were obviously stupid, and yet their greedy little eyes looked at her with a cold contempt when she brought them their cabbage-leaves. As for the cats, there was no possibility of keeping in their good graces—they would walk away in the middle of a conversation. And now all these animals, their likes and their fads, their brushes and combs and tins of flea-powder, must be considered seriously: they were no longer her playmates and Delia's responsibility.

David had gone—and there was an end to adventure; but with Delia's going something far more serious had happened, for now she must put away her "other" life. Lucy said a silent farewell in her heart to the Armenians, not without a certain relief, for of late their tyranny had grown oppressive. But from some of the others it was difficult to part. Where are you now, Lady Isabelle, Queen Bertha and sad Blue Lady, gay Young Acrobat and the Innocent Child? Why do you wring your pale hands? You are fading, but oh, so reluctantly! Yet you have held the stage long enough and you are nothing but a pack of impostors.

The last morning is here, and there are Delia's school clothes—the blue serge coat, rather long to allow for growing, and the panama hat waiting to be put on. Her new umbrella and tennis racquet are strapped importantly together. The men clump upstairs in their heavy boots to carry down the trunk, and Delia fastens the key on a piece of black velvet ribbon, hung round her neck and tucked in to her waist.

They all troop down the lane to the railway halt. Mrs. Bound, the station-mistress, has been told overnight to stop the train; not indeed that she did not know weeks ago that Miss Delia is going to school on this day. Beedles is there already, having taken down the luggage on a hand-cart: he and Mrs. Bound are wrapped in a discussion on the best treatment of broody hens. Mrs. Bound is kind and bustling, and sells Mrs. Gwyn and Delia tickets as far as the next station, where they can buy their tickets for London. They all admire her wallflowers and her early peas and she brings chairs out of the house for them to sit on. They read the advertisements of Sheep Dips—which have beautiful names like "Early Sunrise"—and the orders for the notification of Swine Fever, and the dogs shiver and whimper because they understand that something awful is about to happen. Suddenly Delia says: "Lucy, you can play with Anna-Josephine if you like—and Henrietta too."

"Oh, Delia, may I? D'you really mean Henrietta?"

But before Delia can reply there is a terrible roar and rattle, Mrs. Bound shouts something which no one can hear, the dogs grow frantic, twisting their leads round everyone's ankles, and there is the train and Beedles heaving the trunk, with the guard's help, into the van. Delia is being kissed by everyone, and then she and her mother are both leaning out of the window and the guard is waving his flag and climbing back into the moving train. It moves slowly at first, then faster, and Lucy remembers the yellow flag and the signal they invented: "Come to me!" If only she could use that now! But it is too late; nothing to do now but stand and wave and wave at the two fluttering white handkerchiefs, and then at the back of the train as it echoes on the iron bridge over the river and winds its way eastwards.

They say good-morning to Mrs. Bound and walk back up the lane. The dogs, unleashed at last, rush delightedly ahead; Louisa keeps sniffing and speaks sharply to Maurice when he draws his stick along the railings with an irritating sound; Beedles pushes the empty hand-cart and says nothing.

Lucy decides to feed the tortoise at once. He doesn't really need feeding, but he is silent and soothing and the greenhouse is a good place to hide in. There is a tub of rain-water in one corner where Jarman keeps a syringe for spraying the vine. Often when the world is black Lucy has found consolation in that creaking implement, causing it to suck up the stagnant water slowly as some drinking dragon and then release it in a burst of bubbles.

Now, to her sad astonishment, there is no joy in tub or syringe. This green retreat, its warm and languorous air scented with cherry-pie, and the sight of the young orange trees, that she and Delia have grown from pips, comfort her no more.

THE END

Ah, where are now the voices
That echoed on those shores?
And where the jolly boatmen
Who dipped their yellow oars?
The sunset lingers in the sky,
But still the changing stream runs by.